THE PERFECT PITCH

INDIANAPOLIS LIGHTNING SERIES BOOK 1

SAMANTHA LIND

SAMANTHALIND.COM

The Perfect Pitch
Indianapolis Lightning Series Book 1
Copyright Samantha Lind 2020
All rights reserved.

Cover Design by *Jersey Girl Design*
Cover image by FuriousFotog - Golden Czermak
Cover Model Chase Ketron
Editing by *All About The Edits*
Proofreading by *Proof Before You Publish*

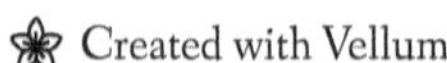 Created with Vellum

CONTENTS

ONE

DEREK

"Mr. Smyth," the judge says, clearing her throat. "I'm going to be very candid with you for a moment. I understand your job puts you and your family in the public eye, and anything and everything you do is under their scrutiny. I also understand that *you* have control over your actions and how you handle yourself when in the public. Your children are of the age that they are impressionable. They worship you and want to be just like Dad. I urge you to take a good hard look at how things have spiraled out of control over the last few years and brought you to this point. I can tell that you still love your soon-to-be ex-wife and kids very much, and this might just be the wake-up call you need to realize what all you've lost."

"Your Honor," I state, clearing my own throat as the emotions of today hit me full force. The pain I'm feeling, sitting at this table across from a judge who is about to tell me how often I can see my two little girls. The two people in this world who mean the most to me. "I know I've fu-messed up," I say, catching myself from dropping the f-bomb in court.

"I promise you"—I look her dead in the eyes, then turn to Jillian, who sits at the table next to mine with her lawyer by her side. I watch as she wipes tears from her cheeks and know I've royally fucked up— "and I promise you, Jillian, that I will do whatever it takes to win the three of you back. To prove that I can change. If that means retiring from the game, so be it. I don't know how I let things spiral out of control to this point, but I will change. I will prove that I can once again be the man you met all those years ago and fell in love with." I sit back and clear my throat. My attorney, James, pats my shoulder from the seat next to me as he gives me his support.

"Since all parties agreed beforehand on the custody arrangements, I don't see any reason to change that. Child support and alimony will be granted to Mrs. Smyth and is to be paid monthly. If there are no objections from Mrs. Smyth or her attorneys, I'll allow that to be handled directly between Mr. and Mrs. Smyth. If any objections, then we can have it paid through the courts."

Jillian's attorney bends her head toward my beautiful wife to talk with her, then says, "No objections, Your Honor."

"Good, good." She jots down some notes on her paperwork. "If no further matters need to be addressed, I'll declare this case closed, and the divorce between Derek Smyth and Jillian Smyth finalized."

"Nothing further, Your Honor," both of our lawyers reply at the same time.

My head drops as the judge bangs her gavel. The finality of that sound and what it means for my future is deafening. How the hell did I allow my life to spiral to this? How did I let the best woman in the world slip through my fingers? How did I fail my girls so much?

"Are you all right?" James asks me a few minutes later. I look up at him as he stands and starts to collect the paperwork he had spread out in front of him during the hearing.

"No," I tell him honestly.

"What can I do to help?"

"Nothing," I reply, knowing the only person who can fix this is me. I'm the only one who can prove to my now ex-wife that when I say something, I mean it and I'll be there for all of them. I don't know how I'll do it, but dammit, I will. I can't lose them for good. I already don't get to see my girls very often with my busy travel schedule as it is. Living without them under the same roof will make it even worse. I look over at Jillian, and the sadness that fills her face tears at my heart. The one she still owns one hundred percent of. She discreetly wipes a tear away as she stands and slings the strap of her purse over her shoulder, then takes the few steps until she's standing in the walkway between the two tables, stopping to look over at me.

"Goodbye, Derek," she says, her voice cracking. We've spent the last ten years together, so I'm sure she's not handling this well. "I'll have the girls packed and ready to go for you to pick them up on Saturday morning. Just text me when you're on your way."

"Okay," I tell her, knowing this is the first step I have to take to prove to her I'm going to change.

I watch as she walks out of the courtroom. The door shuts behind her and I sink back into the chair. "Let's get out of here," James says. "The next hearing starts in ten minutes."

I stand and follow him from the courtroom. Once I'm in the hall, I look around to see if Jillian is still here, but I don't see her anywhere. I don't know why she'd stick around; it isn't like this is a place either of us want to be.

TWO

JILLIAN

"M᷒ommy, Mommy!" my four-year-old, Addison, calls from my bedroom door. I roll over and look at the clock to find it's one-minute past six.

"What, Addy?" I ask, patting the empty space next to me on my giant king-size bed. She hops up on the bed and burrows under the covers.

"I couldn't fall back to sleep," she tells me once settled in next to me. "I wanted to snuggle with you, Mommy."

"You can always snuggle with me, baby girl." I pull her closer to me, burying my nose in her mop of curls, and breathe in her little girl smell.

"When will Daddy be here?" she asks quietly, a few moments later.

"After breakfast."

The ink has only been dried on our divorce paperwork for three days, but it was a long time coming, if I'm really being honest with myself. Derek let the fame of being a starting pitcher in the MLB get to his head and in the way of what should have been his priorities—our two daughters and me. I'm not trying to be a bitch and say I'm more important than his career, but he was always out doing stupid shit and getting himself into trouble.

When I first met him, freshman year of college for both of us, he was this laid-back, easygoing guy. He flirted and charmed me for months before I gave in to him and finally agreed to our first date. That was all it took for me to hand over my heart.

"I miss Daddy," she states, the longing for him evident in her voice, and I bite back tears. As much as it killed me to file for divorce, I did it for my girls. I needed them to see they should be first in their future husbands' lives, not second, third, fourth behind his career, or booze, or the spotlight. As much as I didn't want to take Derek away from them the little amount of time he was home, I knew it had to be done.

So, a year ago, I filed for divorce. We agreed he would stay in the house until closer to things being finalized, and yet things didn't really change. He still partied and did the shit I told him needed to change if he had any desire for us to stay together. I was done being second to everything else in his life.

The look on his face this past week when we went to court killed me. The look he gave me when he addressed the judge and me, gave me a fleeting spark of hope this was the kick in the pants he needed to get his shit together and realize he's got more important things at home rather than going out and partying it up with his teammates all the time. I love his best friend, JJ, but the man is a horrible influence on Derek. I'd never tell him he can't spend time with him, but it would be nice for both of them to grow up and act their ages.

"I know you do, Addy. But you'll get to see him later today and spend the night with him at his new house. That sounds exciting, doesn't it!?" I ask her, trying to make her excited about our situation.

"I guess so," she says on a sigh, as only a four-year-old can.

"Help!" I hear another soft voice fill my room as my other daughter, Penelope, tries to climb up onto my bed. "Mommy, I needs help!" she states matter-of-factly in all her three-year-old sass. I roll over and reach down, grabbing Penny by the armpits to haul her up onto the bed.

"Scooch over," I tell Addy, so I can move closer to the center of the bed. With one of my girls on each side of me, their heads resting on my shoulders, we snuggle in under the covers. I reach over to the nightstand for the remote control. "How about some cartoons?"

"Yes!" They both cheer as we wait for the TV to turn on and the channel guide to pop up. I scroll through the options, deciding on Disney Jr. for them. We settle in for the rest of the current show and another episode before I start to hear their tummies growling.

"How about some chocolate chip pancakes before Daddy picks you up?" I ask the girls.

Penny's eyes light up. "With bacon?" A girl after my own heart.

"Sure, why not?" I tell her, sitting up and blowing a raspberry on her exposed belly, and she giggles.

We all head out into the living room, and I flip the TV on for them before I head to the kitchen where I pull out all the ingredients to make their favorite pancakes and bacon. Having been a stay-at-home mom since Addison was born, I've gotten used to making as much for them as I can from scratch. Top that off with Penny's allergies, and it just makes things easier for me, knowing exactly what is going into her food.

Breakfast passes us by in a whirl of flour, chocolate chips, sprinkles, and syrup. By the time they're finished, my kitchen is a mess, but so worth the time it will take me to clean it all up. My girls will only be little for so long, and I'm determined not to let this time in their lives pass me by.

"Go get dressed, Daddy will be here shortly," I tell the girls once I have them cleaned up from breakfast.

"I've got your bags all ready for him, so all you have to worry about is what you want to wear today."

They both are independent and have a mind of their own when it comes to getting dressed, so I just let them be. It isn't worth the fight with two headstrong little girls. I learned early to pick my battles, and clothes is not one I choose to fight over yet. Now, when they're older and I'm not the one picking out everything they wear, that might be a different story.

While the girls are in their rooms getting dressed, I get started on cleaning the kitchen. I hear my phone buzz against the counter. Picking it up, I see a text from Derek.

Derek: On my way, I'll be there in ten minutes or so. Need a coffee or anything?

Jillian: See you then, girls are just getting dressed. They've had breakfast, so they should be ready to go until lunchtime. And thanks, but I'm good.

I set my phone down and go to double-check that their bags are by the front door. Having never done this whole "hand off my kids to my ex-husband" thing, I don't know what to expect.

"Daddy, Daddy!" Addy and Penny come running and screaming through the halls when they hear the doorbell chime nearly ten minutes later, on the dot. It's weird to know Derek is on the other side of the door, and I'm sure it's weird for *him* to be standing out there, waiting for me to open the door for him. We bought this house shortly after he was acquired by the Lightning. We knew we wanted to have a family one day and as soon as I saw this house, I knew it was the one. When I asked for the divorce, it was one of the few things I requested to keep. I wanted to keep the girls in the only home they've ever known, and near their friends and preschool.

"Hello," I greet Derek as I open the door, and he hands over a Starbucks cup before he drops down to the girls' level and opens his arms up wide as they both jump onto him at the same time. He stands, holding them both up as he hugs them tight. It's this man I miss the most. The family-oriented man who I fell in love with. The one I wish was still here on a daily basis.

"Hi," he says finally, looking at me once he's given each girl a kiss, then sets them down between the two of us.

"Are you all set up for them?" We haven't talked much since he moved out last weekend. "And thank you for this," I tell him, holding up the coffee he brought me.

"Mostly. I was going to take them to Target and let them pick out their own bed sets today, as well as some toys to keep at my place." He lifts his baseball cap off his head and runs his fingers through his hair. Unlike a lot of professional pitchers who grow their hair out long, Derek has always kept his on the shorter side. "And you're welcome. I hope it's still your favorite," he says sheepishly.

"I'm sure they'll love that." I look down at our daughters. "I picked up an extra set of EpiPens for Penny, for you to keep at your place. I figured that would be easier than making sure we transfer them back and forth. I also included a list of all her safe brands and brands to avoid for you. Don't hesitate to call me if you aren't sure."

"Jill, I've got it. I know what our daughter can and can't have," he says sharply.

I smack my forehead. "Sorry, of course you do. I just worry about her," I tell him honestly.

While I know Derek would never do anything purposely to put Penny in harm's way, I just worry some-times he isn't as vigilant as I am with her. It only takes one slip-up and the next thing you know, she's unable to breathe and requiring an ambulance and trip to the emergency room.

"What time do you think you'll bring them home tomorrow night?" I see the girls are starting to get antsy standing between us, so I grab shoes for both of them and drop down to my knees to help them both get them on.

"I hadn't really decided on a specific time. Would after dinner work? I can bring them back in jammies and ready for bed. Maybe stick around and help with bedtime. Or bring them back after dinner and do bath and jammies here, then help get them into bed?" he asks, and I can see the hope in his eyes.

"I'm sure they would love that. Either way is fine with me. Just give me a heads-up so I'm home when you're ready to come over."

"Got a hot date?" he asks, a smirk on his lips.

"Nope," I tell him, popping the P. "Unless you consider my Netflix account and bottle of wine a hot date. But, I figured with the girls out of the house and with you, I should get as many of my errands out of the way as I can, and get grocery shopping for the week done. Normal weekend things that take twice as long when I have these two with me."

I pulled both girls into a hug. "Be good for Daddy," I tell them both, kissing them on the cheek before I let them go. "Here are their bags. Call me if you need anything."

"We'll be fine," he says, giving me a pointed look, then turns to the girls. "Won't we, girls?"

He bends down and sweeps both of them up into his arms. With both of their backpacks hanging off his forearms and a child in each arm, I watch from the doorway as my heart walks out of my house. I watch as he loads the girls into his truck, making sure to buckle each one in their seats, and I bite my lower lip to hold back the sob that threatens to escape my lips as he backs out of the driveway.

Once his truck is gone, I head back inside and close the door behind me. I slide down the door until my ass hits the ground and sob into my t-shirt until my tears run dry.

When there are no more left in me for now, I hoist myself up, pull up my imaginary big girl panties, and head for the shower.

THREE

DEREK

"I love this one, Daddy!" Penny says as she stands in front of a bed set with a unicorn on it.

"Okay, if that's the one you want, I'll put it into the cart."

"It is! I love it already!" she tells me. I find the design in a twin-size package and toss it into my cart.

"What about you, Addy? What one do you want?"

"I don't know," she says, looking at all the options. She's always been our indecisive child, taking forever to make a decision sometimes. I drop down to her level and pull her into my side.

"What ones are you thinking about?" I ask her, dropping a kiss to the top of her head.

"I just want you to come home. Why do you have to live at a different house?" she asks, her little bottom lip trembling as she turns into me and starts bawling. *Fuck.*

"I'm so sorry, Addison. Daddy is going to do everything he can to make things right with Mommy, but for now, this is the way things have to be, okay, sweetheart? Daddy and

Mommy love you and Penny very much, and that will never change, okay? You girls did nothing wrong. Sometimes mommies and daddies need a break from each other to work things out. Sometimes they are better off living in different houses and sometimes they can live together, but no matter where we live, we will always love you and your sister with all our hearts."

"Okay." She hiccups as she works to calm herself down as her tears start to dry up. I wipe her cheeks off and kiss her forehead. "I like the purple one," she tells me, pointing to a bed set that has a purple background and a large rainbow in the center of it.

"This one?" I ask, pulling it off the shelf and holding it up in front of her. She nods her head, so I toss it into the cart along with the other one. "How about the matching sheet sets to go with the blankets?" I ask my girls and they both jump up and down excitedly.

After finding the matching sheets, we end up adding the decorative pillows, a bedside lamp for each of them, and some wall decorations. As I told Jillian, I want them to feel like my condo is home for them when they're with me, so whatever it will take to do just that is what will happen.

"How about we head to the toy section?" I ask once we've filled the cart with bedding and accessories.

"Yes!" Addison calls out as she leads the way. "Daddy, can we go to the American Girl store?" she sweetly adds, stopping to look at me with her puppy dog eyes.

I have a hard time saying no to my girls, but I also can't spoil them too much or Jill will kill me. "We'll see." I know she won't forget, but at least, for now, it pushes off the question until later. "Let's pick out a few things here, for now," I tell both of them as we arrive in the toy section.

I allow them to each pick out a handful of things, then

head for the shelving department to grab some bins for them to store everything in. When I signed the lease a couple weeks ago on my condo, I went to the nearest furniture store and bought a bedroom set for my room, along with a bed, dresser, and nightstand for each of the girls, and then some living room furniture. Everything was delivered last week, but I left their rooms bare so they could help me fill them up.

"Are you girls ready for some lunch?" I ask after loading them into the truck, then emptying the two carts full of bags we ended up with on our stop at Target.

"I'm starving!" Penny tells me from her seat behind me.

I smile at her reflection in the rearview mirror. "Me too, Penny girl."

"What do you girls want to eat?" I ask as I clip my own seatbelt on and put my truck into drive.

"Pizza!" Addison calls out just as Penny yells, "Chicken nuggets!"

"Hmmm..." I say, loud enough for both of them to hear, trying to work out a compromise. "How about Chick-fil-A for lunch and then we can order pizza for dinner?"

"Can we play after we eat?" Addison asks.

"If you want to," I tell her, pulling out on the road. I drive the few miles to the nearest Chick-fil-A and take us inside, ordering what I know the girls and I like to eat. This is also a place Jillian brings the girls regularly, so it's safe for Penny to eat. I know I snapped at her when she started going on about Penny's allergies, and I realize she's just worried. While I'll admit I might not have been the most observant, I'm not going to give my kid something she can't have that could potentially kill her.

"Finish up your food, Penny girl, and then you can go play for a little bit," I tell her a short while later, as I wait for her to slowly eat. Addison finished eating about ten minutes ago already and has been playing away. Thankfully, they have large glass windows, so I can see her just fine as I sit here with Penny.

"Daddy, I've missed you," Penny finally tells me as she takes another bite of her nugget.

"I miss you, too, baby girl." I pull her into my lap and drop a kiss to the top of her head. The girls are used to me being away when I'm on the road for games, sometimes a few nights at a time, but this is different, and we all know it. "Are you full? Do you want to go play with your sister before it's time to go?"

"No, I stay with you," she tells me, as she twists her body around and wraps her arms around my neck. I have to bite back the emotions that threaten to spill out of me at my three-year-old's words. My girls might be young, but they are damn perceptive. I didn't realize until Addison's outburst in Target, and now Penny's, how much this entire situation is affecting them. It's a huge blow to my heart, and someone might as well take a baseball bat to it with the way it's feeling right about now.

"How about we head to Daddy's house and unpack everything. Get your bed set up and toys out," I suggest.

"Okay, Daddy," she agrees. I slide out of the booth, Penny still in my arms, as I walk the two steps to the door of the play area.

"Addy, time to go," I call into the small room.

"But, Daaaaaaaaddy." She exaggerates my name. "Penny didn't play with me yet," she whines as she comes down from the structure and over to where I'm standing.

"I know, bug, but Penny is ready to leave. She doesn't want to play today, so we're going to head home and go get your new beds set up. How does that sound?" I ask once I've crouched down to her level.

"Okay," she says dramatically.

If this is her attitude at four years old, lord help us when she's a teenager. I stand up and grab her hand, and it's then I notice the moms who are hanging around in the play area. They're not so subtly watching *me* and not their children. *Fuck.* I really hope my little chat with my daughter doesn't end up on TMZ, like my last drunken night at a bar did a few weeks ago. We return to our table and clean up before heading back out to my truck.

A couple hours later, the girls and I have everything from Target unpacked, washed, and their beds made. I've opened all their toys and put together the few that required assembly. With them playing away in the living room, I grab my phone and snap a few pictures of them.

> **Derek:** All's well, Addison had a little meltdown in Target that I'll fill you in on tomorrow and Penny had a rough few moments when we had lunch, but all seems well now. They want pizza for dinner, anything I should be aware of when ordering to make sure it's safe for Penny?

I shoot off the quick text to Jillian, along with a couple of the pictures I snapped of the girls. I know this is hard on her. I could tell she was holding back her emotions when I was leaving her house with them this morning.

> **Jillian:** Aww, looks like the three of you are having a good time. They're going to love those bed sets. I'm sorry they've both had some rough moments, they've

had a few here as well. For pizza, stick to Joe's. Just tell them when you call that it's a pizza for Penny and they'll make sure to make it on a clean pan to avoid cross contamination and won't put the egg wash on. They know us well enough so it shouldn't be a problem. I can call it in for you if you want, just let me know. And thanks for checking with me. I know you can handle it, but I'm always here to help.

Derek: Thanks for the offer. If I run into any issues, I'll let you know. See you tomorrow, probably around 6/6:30ish.

Jillian: Anytime. Enjoy your time together, and I'll see you all tomorrow.

I toss my phone aside, making a mental note to call in our pizza order in an hour or so. Jillian has done a great job with them over the past four years and one thing that has helped is keeping them on a somewhat strict schedule. I don't need to go fucking that up when they get to come spend time with me, so my plan is to stick to it as best as I can. If I'm going to win my family back, I've got to start small and show Jillian I really do care and I'm all-in. Not that I wasn't before, but I just had a really shitty way of showing it. Those days are over. I'm turning over a new leaf and making these girls number one, just as they always should have been.

"Daddy, can we play dress up?" Penelope asks a little while later.

"Sure can, baby girl. Go bring me what you want to put on," I tell her.

One of the things they picked out was a chest full of

dress-up clothes. Since it's one of their favorite things to do, I figured it was a great thing for them to have here at my place. I help Penelope into a dress, along with a tiara and some plastic heels. Once she's all dressed up, Addison is right in on the action, as well. Soon, I have two beautiful little girls all dressed up, and I watch as they prance around my living room. It's been awhile since I've devoted this much one-on-one time with them, and it really brings into perspective just how shitty a father and husband I've been the last couple of years. Just how much I let them and Jillian down with my selfish behavior.

"Are you girls hungry yet?" I ask awhile later. It's already almost five, so I need to get our pizza order called in. With it being the offseason, I'm more lenient on what I eat. During the season, I'm pretty strict and that means not much pizza for me.

"Yes. We're having pizza, right, Daddy?" Addison asks as she comes over to me, needing help out of her dress.

"Yep. I'm going to call it in now. Mommy told me where to order it from so Penny can have it with us."

"Yay! Pizza!" she cheers.

"What do you want on your pizza?"

"Cheese!" they both say at the same time.

"That's all? No meat or anything else?"

"Yuck!" they both state, again in unison, and I laugh at their antics.

"Alrighty then, I'll order you two ladies a cheese pizza and a meat lover's for Daddy. How does that sound?" I ask as I pull them into my arms.

"Blow a raspberry on my belly, Daddy!" Penny cries out as she lifts her shirt. I rub my chin against her exposed skin, tickling her with my short beard. "That tickles!" She squeals in laughter as she tosses her head back and tries to get away from me. I've got her firmly held against my body with my arm around her back, and I lower my lips to her skin, blowing as she first requested. "D-d-d-addy!" she stutters as she laughs, big, huge belly laughs.

"Yes, princess?" I ask, my lips still against her skin.

"Do it again!" she cries, and I oblige her request, blowing another raspberry against her belly.

We continue this cat-and-mouse game for another minute or so before I let my girls go and get up to order the pizza. Just as Jillian said, Joe's knew what I meant when I said that we needed a safe pizza for Penelope. They assured me they were knowledgeable with handling food allergies and would make sure the kids' pizza was perfectly safe for her to eat.

With the pizza ordered, I go back to my girls, who have moved on from dress up to playing with the dolls they picked up at Target. I look around my living room and all I see is pink, frilly girl shit. It looks like the little girl aisle puked in my living room. That's basically what happened. I have a super hard time telling them no, so if it was something they wanted, I didn't really have the heart to deny them today. That might make me an idiot, as kids will pick up on that very quickly, then expect things later. Jillian nor I want our girls to grow up spoiled and entitled brats. They might not ever want for anything, thanks to my professional career and the amount I get paid to throw a baseball, but that doesn't mean they were born with a silver spoon in their mouths, either.

I'm sitting, just watching the girls play, when my phone buzzes from the end table next to me. I grab it and see my little sister, Riley, is calling. There's a decent age gap between the two of us. She's just graduated college this past spring.

"Hey!" I greet as I answer her call.

"Hi. How's it going?"

"It's going. I've got the girls here with me for our first weekend in my new place. What are you up to?"

"Eh, not much. Just having a quiet night in. Can we FaceTime so I can talk to the girls?"

"Sure," I tell her and pull my phone down to accept her FaceTime call.

"You look like crap," she states, once my face fills the screen.

"Thanks? You sure know how to make a guy feel good about himself," I tease, knowing she's just giving me a hard time.

"Things will get better. I have faith in you, Derek."

"It's going to. I need my family back. This entire situation sucks. Both girls had mini breakdowns today because of it and it damn near broke my heart," I tell my sister honestly.

"Speaking of my nieces, where are they?" she asks.

"Addison, Penelope! Aunt Ry wants to FaceTime with you!" I call out to them. "They must have gone into their room to play or get something else," I tell her as I listen for them to come running.

"RyRy!" Penelope calls out as she jumps up onto my lap, hitting my arm and nearly causing me to drop my phone.

"Penny-benny. How are you?" Riley asks her, using the nickname only she calls Penny.

"I's good," Penny answers, adjusting so she's filling the camera area. "RyRy, I got a new blanket today! And toys for Daddy's house."

"That sounds like fun! What color is it?"

"It has a unicorn! Wanna see it?" she asks my sister as

she hops off my lap and steals my phone. She takes off running toward their room, the phone jostling all over the place as she goes.

"Wow, that's awesome! I wish I could have one like that!" Riley tells her as she tries to see what Penny is attempting to show her.

"Aunt Ry, look at mine!" Addison butts in, snatching the phone from Penny's hand and showing off her new bed set.

"I love it! Maybe I can come visit and we can have a sleepover together."

"Yes!" both girls cheer.

"Daddy, Aunt RyRy is coming!" Penelope tells me excitedly.

"I don't think she's coming right now, baby girl. She said maybe when she comes next, you girls could have a sleepover."

She pouts. "Oh."

"Hey! No pouting now. I'll figure out a time I can come visit. I miss my two favorite girls!" Riley says, cheering up both of them.

"We miss you," Addison tells her.

"I know you do, and I miss both of you so much! Look at how big both of you are getting! Stop growing, would you, please?" she teases them.

Penny laughs. "We can't."

"I know, I know." Riley laughs right along with them.

I sit back and just listen in as my girls talk with my sister. Our relationship has definitely grown over the past few years. With our seven-year age gap, we've not always been that way.

"Hey, Ry, we're going to have to cut this call short as the pizza guy just buzzed my apartment."

"I should get going myself. But it was so great to see all of you. Call me if you need someone to talk to," she says to me.

"Will do. Love you, Ry," I tell my sister before hanging up and heading to answer the door.

FOUR
JILLIAN

Showered and dressed, I look around my quiet house. The lack of noise is a little eerie. I hardly ever get time to myself, so this is going to take time to get used to it. I head back into my bathroom and take my hair out of the towel. I might as well take myself out to dinner tonight. Enjoy my new freedom. Most of my friends all have kids and husbands of their own, so it won't surprise me if they all have Saturday night plans already, but I shoot a group text to both my best friend, Tara, and my sister, Mariah.

> **Jillian:** Want to go out for dinner? I'm kid free and need out of the house. I've showered and put on actual clothes. About to put on some makeup and actually do my hair.

They'll both understand what a big deal all of that means as I can usually be found in a t-shirt, yoga pants, my hair up in a ponytail or messy bun on the top of my head, and not a stitch of makeup to be seen. I'm not the prissy—aka Instagram-perfect—professional athlete wife that so many are. Though, I guess now I'm technically no longer a wife of a professional athlete, so I need to get those thoughts out of my mind. I don't think for one minute the few paparazzi who've followed me in the past to snap pictures as I've been out and about won't continue to do so now that Derek and I aren't married. It irritates me when I'm doing something with the girls, as they didn't ask for this type of lifestyle. Not that all the other wives don't go through what we have, but it comes with the territory of Derek being one of the starters. He's in the limelight more, plus, his actions as of late have attracted extra paparazzi to town.

Mariah: I'll gladly run away from home for the evening. Tell me when and where and I'll be there, waiting for you to start drinking, so take an Uber so we can get our drink on.

Jillian: I have no plans of getting wasted, but a drink or two will be consumed.

Mariah: You deserve a night to unwind. Maybe find yourself a hot guy to take home for the night. :winky face: If anyone deserves a wild night filled with no-strings-attached sex, it's you.

Jillian: I'm not interested in a one-night stand, so don't even go there tonight. And no trying to fix me up with anyone either.

Tara: Some good dick would do you some good. And you know what they say, the best way to get over someone is to get *under* someone else.

Jillian: What is this, gang up on Jill day?

Tara: No, the opposite. We're looking out for your best interest. When was the last time you got some good dick? Like, fireworks going off, sweat-slicked bodies, can't catch your breath nor walk the next day type fucking? I agree with Mariah, you need some good dick in your life.

Jillian: Sigh. So, are you free tonight?

Tara: For you, I'm free. Let me just break the news to Adam that he's on kid duty and that I'm going out.

Jillian: Do either of you have a suggestion on where we should meet? I can be ready in twenty or so minutes.

Mariah: My suggestion is downtown. We can start at St. Elmo's and then hit up some bars in the area as we see fit.

Tara: Sounds good to me. Meet you there in an hour, I need time to shower and change. I haven't left the house all day and need to wash the kids off of me.

Jillian: Works for me.

Mariah: See you both then. I'll call and see if we can get on the list now for a table.

Jillian: Probably a good idea. It is a Saturday
night, after all.

I pull up a playlist saved to my phone and get back to
applying some makeup. I don't go overboard since I don't
usually wear any with being home all the time and not
really having anywhere, I go on a regular basis that requires
me to be all made up. Once I'm happy with the reflection in
the mirror, I spritz on some perfume, straighten my top, and
head for the kitchen. I down a small glass of water, then
grab my keys, phone, and purse, and head for the garage. I'm
so used to having two little ones to get loaded and buckled, I
almost feel like I'm forgetting something. I know they're
safe and happy with Derek. If I think about the three of
them too much, I'll lose it and start crying, and God knows
I've cried enough tears over that man. Making the decision
to end our marriage wasn't something I did lightly. I stressed
over the decision for months. But I needed to be strong for
my girls and show them I'm strong and did this for everyone's best interest. That doesn't mean it doesn't hurt, or that
it wasn't a difficult choice.

I get lost in listening to the radio as I make my way
downtown to the restaurant where Tara suggested we start.
I've been here a few times before, so I find it easily. Thankfully, parking is a breeze as another car is pulling out just as
I pull in. Once parked, I check my reflection in the small
mirror in my visor, then grab my purse and step out of my
car. Inside, I find Mariah waiting with a small square pager
in her hands.

"Hey, have you been here long?" I ask as I come up to
stand next to her.

"Just a couple of minutes. They said they should have
our table ready in the next five to ten minutes."

I look around the packed restaurant. "That's not so bad."

"I didn't think so, either. How did today go?" she asks, and I blow out a big breath.

"Okay, I guess. Kind of weird."

"I can only imagine. Was he a dick?" she bluntly asks.

"Not at all. The complete opposite, actually. Texted on his way, offered to bring me coffee, which I declined but he brought anyways. He was short a few times when I reminded him of P's allergies, but I also have to remember that he *is* their dad and while he might not do things the way I do, he's still a good dad and won't do anything on purpose to harm them."

"I'm sure it will be weird the first few times but will become easier to hand the girls back and forth," she reassures me.

"I hope so," I reply as Tara joins us. We chat about our days for a few minutes while we wait for our buzzer to go off.

"To being single and ready to find some new dick!" Tara calls out, holding up a shot glass of vodka. I hold up my own, trying to shush her as I see multiple people around us at the bar turn to look at us. We clink glasses and I quickly shoot the shot down.

"God, that was horrible. I haven't taken a shot like that in years," I tell her, then pucker my lips once more at the aftertaste.

"Evening, ladies. Can I buy you a round?" a guy asks as he tries to join our circle.

"That depends…" Tara says, looking him up and down. "What do you expect to come of buying us a drink tonight?"

"Ummm…" He stalls, obviously trying to think on his feet as to what answer she's looking for. "Nothing, just want to help three beautiful ladies celebrate whatever it is they're out celebrating tonight."

"If you're sure, then, yes, we'll accept a drink. But that's it. None of us will be going home with you or accompanying you to the bathroom for a quick fuck or blowjob."

"Yes, ma'am," he says, turning to flag the bartender down.

Once our free drinks are in hand, the guy bids us goodbye, getting the hint none of us are open to more.

"I can't believe he went through with actually buying us a round," Mariah says, laughing into her martini.

"He was pretty cute," Tara adds, then points at me. "He looked like he could have rocked your world tonight."

"Not interested," I remind her as I finish off my own martini. "I'm going to be in so much pain in the morning."

I set my glass down on the bar top, then flag down one of the bartenders and order a bottle of water to help flush some of the alcohol out of my system.

"Down some water, take a few ibuprofens when you get home, and sleep it all off. When are the girls coming back?" Tara asks.

"Derek said he'd bring them by sometime between six and six thirty."

"Perfect. You have all day to recover," she says, attempting to hand me another shot glass.

"No, no. I'm done for the night," I tell her, pushing the shot glass away from me.

"Come on, live a little!" both of them say in unison as they hold up their own shots and place mine in front of me.

I look down at my watch and see it's already pushing midnight.

"When was the last time you let loose and did whatever the fuck you wanted?" Mariah asks.

"I can't even remember." I bite my bottom lip as I look around the bar.

"Then let go, Jill. You deserve a night to forget. To let loose. To enjoy being a single, twenty-something woman."

"You mean a single, divorced mom of two toddlers, who has no job?"

"Tonight, though, you have no demands. Unless this shot can be looked at as a demand. You have no little ones depending on you. No ex-husband to worry about what he's out doing. It's time that you stopped thinking about everyone else and put yourself first. So, here, take this and *let go.*"

"Fine," I say, accepting the shot glass and downing it.

Everything else in my life has gone to shit. I might as well enjoy tonight.

FIVE

DEREK

"Are you ready to go see Mommy?" I call down the hall to my girls. They were picking up their toys we bought yesterday and making sure they had everything that needs to go back with them.

"Yes!" they both yell as they come barreling down the hallway. I change my stance, in case they don't stop in time—I don't need them toppling me over and potentially hurting one or all of us in the process—but they both skitter to a stop just in front of me.

"Are you still staying to read us bedtime stories?" Penelope asks.

"Sure am, bug," I tell her, picking them both up in my arms. It's a good thing I work out on the regular, as they are both getting big. It won't be long before I can't lift them both at the same time. "How many stories do you think we should read tonight?"

"Five!" she calls out with a giggle.

"Five! That's a lot of stories. What do you say?" I turn my head to Addison.

"Umm, how about seven?!" she exclaims.

"Seven! That's even more than your sister suggested. How about we read as many as we have time for. You girls need to go to bed on time. You have preschool tomorrow. But until then, let's get packed up. Go get your shoes on." I plant a kiss on each of their foreheads before setting them back down on their feet.

"Everyone ready?" I ask a couple minutes later. I've grabbed their overnight bags Jillian packed for them, and now just need to load them up into my truck.

"I'm ready," Penny says, hopping up off the floor where she was sitting, putting her shoes on.

"Daddy, I need help," Addison tells me as she struggles to get her shoes on.

"Stand up and place your foot on Daddy's knee." I offer my hand to help her up. She accepts and stands before me, placing her foot on my knee as I instructed. I fix the shoe, allowing her foot to slip inside of it before I secure the strap.

"Ok, girls, let's hit the road," I tell them, opening up the door for us to walk out of. I quickly get them loaded, placing their bags between the two car seats in the back seat of my truck. "We're going to stop at the store and pick up dinner, then we'll go to Mommy's house."

"Can we get ice cream?" Penny asks as I drive down the street.

"Maybe. Let's see how well you behave as I get the other items we need," I say over my shoulder.

Once at the grocery store, I grab a few meals from the Chinese counter. This was always one of our go-to "we don't feel like cooking" or "let's stay in and have a date night after the kids are in bed" kind of meals.

"How about we bring Mommy some pretty flowers?" I ask as we walk past the florist section.

"Yes!" they both agree. "I think she'll like these ones," Addison adds, pointing at a big arrangement.

"Do you both like that one?" I ask the girls. I don't really think it matters which one we get, as she'll just enjoy receiving them in general. I realize I didn't buy or send her flowers nearly enough while we were married, but I guess that's just one more thing I can add to my list of things I need to work on as I win her back.

They agree on the one bouquet, so I add it to my cart. Before I direct us to the checkout, I stop and grab a bottle of Jill's favorite wine, and then to the ice cream section to let the girls pick some for after dinner. "Okay, girls, let's go. Time to go have some dinner with Mommy."

We make our way over to the self-checkout and they help me scan the items. They love getting to help, so I hand them each a twenty to feed into the machine once I'm ready to pay. They get an even bigger kick when the machine spits out the change and receipt a moment later. In no time, we're back in the truck and on the road again.

"Mommy!" our girls call out as soon as Jill answers the door. My hands are full, between the bags and flowers from the grocery store, and their belongings.

"Hi, my babies!" she greets them, dropping down to her haunches to pull them into her arms. They both latch on to her neck, not seeming to want to let her go. You'd think they hadn't seen her in a month, not a mere thirty some-odd hours later.

"Mommy, we missed you!" Penny tells her.

Jill kisses her on the forehead. "I missed you, too, Pen."

"I don't mean to interrupt this moment, but can I come in? My hands are a bit full and I don't want to drop anything."

"Oh, of course!" Jillian says, standing and moving the

girls to the side so I can slip by them. I head for the kitchen, setting the bags of food down as I open the cabinet where I know she keeps the vases. I add some water, then place the bouquet inside.

"These are for you. The girls picked them out just for you when we stopped at the store for dinner," I tell her, winking at my girls.

"Oh, did they now?" she asks, leaning in to smell the flowers. "They sure are pretty and smell amazing."

"I'd have to agree, just like all of you," I state, making sure she damn well knows it.

Jillian is the quintessential girl-next-door, every teenage boy's wet dream. She's got that natural beauty you can't replicate with any amount of makeup. She can pull off a ratty old t-shirt and yoga pants or a designer dress and heels that cost thousands of dollars. It was one of the many things that drew me to her when we first met in college. I was the tall, skinny, hadn't quite grown into myself yet, baseball-playing jock. She made me work for it, but man, was she worth the chase.

I still remember the first time I saw her from across the quad that first month of freshman year. She walked by with a group of her floormates. Her caramel-colored hair blowing in the slight breeze. She had on skintight jeans, and a tank top that did little to hide her curves. All I know is I almost fell off the bench I was sitting at with some of the guys from my team. They gave me shit about it for weeks. It took me another two weeks to find out her name and a few fucking *months* before she agreed to go out on a date with me.

"So, did you have a good time while we were gone?" I ask, changing the subject.

"You could say that," she says, a slight blush creeping up her cheeks.

"Wild night?" I ask, jokingly.

"You could say that," she repeats, her blush deepening. *Fuck. Please don't tell me she was out fucking some random dude.* "I met Mariah and Tara downtown for dinner and drinks. They encouraged me to let loose and enjoy my night of freedom. After a few drinks, I finally gave in and we might have closed down the bar. I've been nursing quite the hangover today," she confesses.

"Sounds like a good night. Did you come back here last night?" I ask, fishing for more information about her *wild night*.

"Yep, we ordered an Uber and I came home. Took some meds before crawling into bed and woke up feeling pretty good, considering. I've had a small headache, but no puking or anything like that. It could have been so much worse than it was. After lunch, Tara and Adam came and picked me up, and he dropped us both off so we could get our cars back home."

"Did you get any of your errands done that you wanted?"

"The important ones, yes. The fridge and pantry are stocked for the week. Everything else can be done while the girls are at preschool this week."

"I don't have anything going on this week, so if you need me to come by and give you a break, just call me," I tell her.

"Thanks, I'll let you know. And you know that you're welcome to come see them or pick them up whenever you want, right? I don't want to keep you from them. That's never been my intention with all of this."

"I know, and I appreciate that," I reply sincerely.

"Are you not training at all this offseason?" she asks.

"I am, but Josh is out of town. He went to visit family for the week. I'm sure I'll hit up the gym and go throw some balls at the cages, but nothing too demanding. I *am* allowed to have some downtime during my off months," I say teasingly. "Speaking of downtime... I was thinking that maybe we could take the girls down to Florida and to D-I-S-N-E-Y-W-O-R-L-D." I spell out the word, so the girls don't overhear. "I was thinking maybe the week after Thanksgiving. I know they'd have to miss preschool, but I figured they're still young enough that missing a few days of school isn't a big deal yet."

"Missing school is fine, but I don't know, Derek." She sighs. "Not many newly divorced couples go on vacation together. Wouldn't that be kind of weird?"

"I don't think it would be. We'd be doing it for the girls. Each getting to spend time with them. Seeing the excitement that it brings to both of them, together. We've got lots of milestones to make it through over their lifetimes, so what's wrong with taking a vacation together as one of those memory-making times? And if you're worried about the money side of things, I'll pay for all of it. I don't expect you to pay for a portion of it out of the child support I'm paying." I pause for a second and give her arm a squeeze. "And you know that if you ever need more, just tell me. I don't want you to have to put the girls into daycare because you have to go back to work. They thrive being at home with you, and that isn't something that I want to take away from the three of you just because I'm no longer living at home and we're no longer married. I still love you, Jillian, and would do anything for you and our girls. I fucked up and I know it, but I'm going to prove to you that I'm changing. The three of you are now my priority. It really fucking sucks that it took me so long to hit rock bottom and realize that. But hearing that judge hit the gavel on her desk was the wake-up call I needed."

I observe Jill's body language as she takes in and digests everything I just word vomited on her. I realize everything I dumped was a shit ton to take in and process, so it doesn't surprise me she's quiet for a few moments.

With her eyebrows furrowed, she really looks at me. I can faintly hear the girls playing in the other room, so thankfully, they aren't listening in on our conversation. "I-I don't really know what to say right now to all of that." She pauses, and takes a deep breath, almost as if she's trying to keep herself calm in this moment.

"You don't have to say anything. Just know I'm going to win you back. You were the best thing to ever happen to me and I want that back. I want to know that when I come home at night, it will be to you. That when I crawl into bed at night, it will be your warm, sexy body that I get to curl around," I tell her as I walk around the island counter that has been separating us, stopping only when I'm standing a foot or so away from her. I reach my hand out and cup her face. My big palm covers the entire side. I sink my fingertips into her hair and swipe my thumb across her plump bottom lip. "And just so you know, you're the only woman who has my eye. We might technically be single, but I can promise you that the next woman I kiss, the next woman I fuck, the next woman I make love to, will be you."

I drop a kiss to her forehead, then step back, breaking the connection. I not only hear but can feel the hitch in Jillian's breath. I'm not sure if it was the declaration or the kiss that I planted on her that caused it, but that one tiny hitch gives me so much hope I'll be successful in winning her back. I just have to stay focused and throw a perfect game, so to speak, to win my girl back.

I've had one perfect game in my professional career. Not many pitchers ever achieve that milestone, so I don't take it for granted one bit. Now to channel that determination into winning Jillian back.

"Shall we eat before the food gets cold?" she asks, obviously still shocked from everything that has transpired over the past few minutes.

"Sounds perfect," I tell her, then call out to the girls. "Pen! Addy! Time to get washed up for dinner."

I can hear their little feet hitting the floor as they both take off for the little bathroom off the dining room to wash up. I pull out four plates—two adult ones and two character ones for the girls—along with forks for all of us. I carry them to the table as Jillian brings the to-go cartons of food with her. "What would you girls like to drink?" I ask as they take a seat at the table.

"I'll grab their cups. Would you like anything?" Jillian asks.

"Just a glass of water will be fine, thanks." I smile at her from across the table. I watch as she turns and walks away . Thank God I'm sitting down and have the table blocking the view of my very tented jeans. There is no hiding the bat in my pants today. My mind briefly wanders to after the girls are in bed. I wonder if I could convince Jillian to let me back into her bed for the night. She looks stressed to the max, and I'm sure an orgasm or five would help her with that. I know damn well it will help me out tonight.

We laugh our way through dinner with the girls. Their antics and silliness are a balm to my soul as I listen to them tell Jillian about our time together. They rat me out on all the things I bought for them at Target yesterday, but she understood me wanting them to have things to just keep at my condo to play with while they are there. No way would I be able to keep them from going crazy at my place without toys to keep them occupied.

With everyone full, I stand and collect the plates and take them to the kitchen. I return to grab the containers of food and Jillian gives me a quizzical look.

"How about you go get the girls in the bath while I clean up and put away the leftovers. Then I'll come help get them ready for bed. I might have promised them I'd read them five books before bed."

"They have you wrapped around their little fingers, you know that, right?" she asks, a shit-eating grin filling her kissable lips.

"I'm aware." I have to keep from leaning forward and capturing her lips with my own in this moment. "I at least shot down taking them to the American Girl store yesterday."

"I'm glad," she says, chuckling. "They don't need another doll or doll accessory right now. Especially not a doll that costs over a hundred dollars. They're three and four."

"But they're my princesses," I defend.

"You keep that attitude up and they'll be spoiled brats by the time they're six. They need limits, Derek," she says, giving me a pointed look. "You can't swoop in and hand them everything on a silver platter. They need to learn that you sometimes have to work to get what you want. Daddy can't always swoop in and buy at that moment."

"Yeah, yeah, yeah. I know. But they're still my little princesses and I can spoil them occasionally. Like, say, the week after Thanksgiving," I reply, giving Jillian my best puppy dog face, I can muster up.

"I'll think about it, okay?" she says finally.

"That's all that I ask but think fast, as that's only a few weeks away and we'll need to get things booked."

"Okay," she says before turning and walking out of the

dining room. I finish clearing off the table and head for the kitchen. A few minutes later, I hear the girls laughing as they splash around in the bathtub, usually electing to take a bath together so they can play. We've really lucked out that they play so well together. Both are headstrong little girls, just like their momma, not that I would have it any other way. But I've got friends whose kids are constantly at each other's throats, so much that the parents are pulling out their hair, stressed over it all the time. So, I thank my lucky stars my girls are the best of friends.

I quickly rinse the dishes and load the dishwasher, then place the small amount of leftovers into a container and set it in the fridge. Before leaving the kitchen, I open the bottle of wine I picked up for Jillian and pour her a decent glass, taking it with me as I go to find my girls.

"How's it going in here? Any water still left in the tub?' I tease the girls. They love to splash, and tonight's no different as I step in a puddle of water.

"Daddy! Of course there's water in the tub. How else would we be splashing it and getting clean?" Addison asks me.

I laugh at their antics. "Just checking, since there seems to be a lot of water outside of the tub."

"Here, this is for you," I tell Jillian as I hand her the glass of wine.

"Thanks." Confusion laces her voice.

"Take it and go take a hot, relaxing bath of your own. I've got them."

She looks over at me like I've grown a second head, but eventually accepts the glass of wine from my hand and stands to follow my instructions.

"Did you bring this?" she asks, stopping at the doorway and looking over her shoulder at me.

"I did. Figured you could use a glass to relax with tonight," I tell her before turning back to the girls.

I can see her reflection in the mirror, and watch her out of my peripheral vision as she takes in my words before finally walking off down the hall toward the master bedroom with an en suite bathroom. I'm still convinced it was that en suite bathroom that made her fall in love with this house when we were house-hunting. Don't get me wrong, it's a great house, but that bathroom was built to be a dream escape. It's practically a mini spa all on its own.

"Are you both wrinkly enough yet?" I ask the girls about ten minutes later. They both hold up their hands that are, in fact, nice and wrinkly from the amount of time in the water. "Looks like it. Let's get out."

I lean over and snag the towels hanging up on the rack. I open one up and wrap it around Penny as she climbs out of the tub, then do the same when Addison clambers out after her a moment later. I help them dry off, making sure to get as much water from their curly hair as I can before following them down the hall and into their room. Jillian has already set out clean undies and pajamas for both of them, so I just help when asked.

Once both are dressed, I take them back into the bathroom where I put my dad skills to the test, spraying their hair with the detangler, and then tackle combing it out. I even manage to get it braided like Jillian does, to keep it from getting super tangled while they sleep.

"Daddy, read this one!" Penny says, shoving a book into my hands once we're back in their room after hair, vitamins, and brushing of teeth.

"Okay, and what other ones?" I ask them both.

"This one, too, Daddy!" Addison says excitedly. "It's my favorite one!"

"All right, let's get tucked into bed and then I'll start reading."

I help get them settled in, give them each a kiss and hug, then make sure their blankets are all snug, just the way they like them. I flip off the overhead light, leaving only the lamp that is between their beds on for me to read by. I grab the floor chair-pillow thing we have and lean back against the wall, diving right into the first book in my pile. At first, the girls laugh along as I read, but as I near the end, I realize they're both quiet. I look over at them as I finish the last page and find them sound asleep. So much for reading five books tonight.

SIX

JILLIAN

I sink into the hot water; the bath bomb I grabbed at the last second fizzing away as it dissolves in the water. The calming scent from it is helping me relax as I slide down until the water is just under my chin. I rest my head back on the headrest as I close my eyes. I have some music streaming quietly through the Bluetooth speakers that are hardwired in the room. The builder of this house really did think of everything when they built this space.

I crack my eyes open when I hear the pitter-patter of feet down the hall as the girls and Derek make their way into their bedroom to get ready for bed. I'm prepared for my bath to be interrupted but am pleasantly surprised when they never come in here, not even to say goodnight. I enjoy the glass of wine Derek brought me, my first sip of it confirming it's my favorite kind. He's been showing me this week that he actually did pay attention to those kinds of details when we were married. Funny how it took a divorce and him moving out for him to start showing me these are things he actually knows.

I still don't know where things went wrong. He was

always very attentive in the early years. The almost-perfect boyfriend, and the attentive husband and father when the girls were first born. But over the years, as more pressure was placed on his shoulders, things started to crack, and he began doing stupid shit that always ended up in the media. They, of course, would spin things to give them the best headlines, no matter how correct it was or wasn't, never taking into consideration what those headlines were doing to him and his family.

I finish off my wine as the water starts to go cold, so I drain the tub and move to the shower, where I quickly rinse off and wash my hair. Once out, I slather on my favorite lotion before slipping into some comfy pajama pants and a t-shirt. I toss my hair up into a messy bun on the top of my head and call it good. I've got no one to impress, and it isn't like Derek hasn't seen me looking like this practically every night for the past six or more years. I make no apologies for being comfortable in my own home at night. If someone doesn't like it, they can see their way out the door.

I finally wander my way out to see if Derek is still here. I find him in the living room, watching a hockey game on TV. He's got the volume down low and is sprawled out, looking comfortable. He's lying on his side, the perfect little spot in front of him I could easily slide into, as I have a thousand times. It makes me long for and miss his arms around me, holding me close to his body. I miss the feel of his warmth as he'd wrap himself around me on the couch or in bed. Always my protector.

Derek must sense my presence and thought process as he looks over at me, then pats the open space in front of him. I know I shouldn't, but the invitation is just so tempting. I'm relaxed and feeling good after that glass of wine and hot bath, so I give in. I walk around the couch and lie down in front of him, melting into his warmth as his front is flush with my back. There's no ignoring the hardness of his erection as it presses against my ass.

Once I'm settled in his embrace, his large hand slides along my hip, his fingertips slipping under my top as he brings his hand to rest against my stomach. His touch is like an electrical current that shoots straight to my core. It's been awhile since we last slept together, and to say I'm missing that intimacy is an understatement. We always had a very healthy sexual relationship. Even after the girls were born, we would find time for each other.

"I've missed this," he whispers next to my ear. "I've missed you. Tell me what you need from me."

I can hear the sincerity and desperation in his voice, and a tear slips from my eye at his words. Why did it take all of this for him to want to change? Why wasn't my asking for it for the year prior to filing for divorce enough to open his eyes to the damage and hurt he was causing our family. I discreetly wipe the tear from my cheek, biting my lower lip to try and keep from full-on crying while he's here tonight. I don't need him to see me break down, because once I do, I don't know that I'll be able to resist him.

"Baby, talk to me," he says, rolling me in his arms to face him. He notices another tear that escaped, and quickly wipes it away with his thumb. He kisses my forehead, and that one movement has me melting into him that much more. His tender side coming out in full force tonight, and quickly sucking me in.

"I miss you so much, but how do I know that you're really going to change? I can't go back to the way things were. The partying, the reckless behavior, isn't you, and it isn't something I want our girls exposed to. They are still young enough to not really know what's going on, but that's going to quickly change."

He cups my face, turning it up until I'm looking him dead in the eyes. "I promise you that I'm done with all of that shit. You, the girls, are my priority. I'd give up baseball if you told me that would get me back here and into this house again. I'd have to figure out how to buy out my contract, but I'd make it happen if that's what it would take."

"I don't want you to quit your job. You have a World Series to win before you can retire," I tease him a little. He's come so damn close but hasn't quite made it to that championship.

"Thank you. As much as it would kill me to quit, I'd do it for you and the girls, and I'm serious about that."

"You're not quitting, so stop that nonsense. I'd *never* ask you to do so, unless it was because of your health or due to an injury. I know that baseball has always been your first love and I'd never ask you to give that up, but, Derek, I can't go back to the drinking and the partying and the days where those things were more important than being home with your family."

"So, what do you need from me?" he asks, resting his forehead against mine.

"I really don't know, besides time and proof. I need to see the change. I need to see you making an effort. I can't tell you how long that will take, but I just need proof, Derek. I know that the man I fell in love with and depended on for so many years is still in there, and he can come back. I know the weight of the team riding on your shoulders has been a burden to carry, and while you might not have dealt with the stress the best way, I hope that with some changes when the season returns, you can learn how to handle it better and keep your family the priority that we should be, and not become second or third on the list."

"I can give you time. I might not like it, but I promise you that I will—no, strike that—I. *Have*. Changed. No more bullshit, no more making you or the girls feel like you're not my top priority. I can't change the amount of time I have to dedicate to them, as you well know, but I can control what I do during my off-time. Now, I'm sure I'll fuck up a time or two, but I promise you that I'm going to put one hundred percent of my efforts into getting you back, and you can mark my words: I *will* wife you up again."

"You're pretty confident about that," I state, raising my eyebrows at him.

"Call me cocky, but I'm confident in my abilities to wear you down. I've done it once and I can do it again. I know all your weak points," he says, dropping his face into my neck and lightly sucking on the skin right below my ear. My skin immediately puckers with goose bumps from my neck straight down to my toes. An involuntary shiver rakes through my body, and as much as I try and hide the effect he has on me, I can't hide the fact my entire body is trembling from his touch.

"You *are* cocky," I say, laughing as I push at his chest.

"I can show you just how cocky." He presses his hips against mine, and I feel as his cock pushes against my center. The friction against my clit has me gasping and wanting more. "Let me make you feel good, baby," he whispers against my skin. "Let me take care of you tonight."

"Derek," I moan. My mind is whirling. I want what he's offering, but I know crossing this line just muddies the water between us.

"Jillian." He says my name like a caress falling from his lips. "You know how good it feels to come on my tongue or cock. How relaxed you'll be afterwards. Just let go and let me make you feel, baby."

He's good, I'll give him that. But I also have one hell of a vibrator that can get the job done in the meantime.

"We can't, Derek," I tell him, finding my backbone and slipping out of his embrace.

I knew lying with him on the couch like this was a bad idea. Now we're both horny and having to use all our strength to keep from ripping each other's clothes off. It'd be so easy to give in to Derek's offer. To let him strip my clothes off and bury his face between my legs. I rub them together, trying to find some relief and finding none. Now, I'm sexually frustrated and shaking my head at how I got myself into this situation. Tara and Mariah are going to have a heyday if I ever confess to what happened tonight.

"I think you should go. I can't do this tonight and I can't trust myself to be around you much longer before I give in to your offer." I stand a few feet from him, my arms wrapped around my torso as a form of armor, in an attempt to protect my heart.

"If that's what you want," he says, dropping his shoulders and resting his elbows on his knees as he leans forward on the couch. His head falls between them as he looks down. In this position, he looks so defeated, and I worry for a split-second that I've crushed him. Then I remember I gave him so many chances to change his behavior before I actually filed for divorce, and it wasn't until it was finalized, he decided to prove to me he was ready to change. Ready to realign his priorities back to what they once were.

"I don't really know what I want right now, but I can't be making any rash decisions that are mostly controlled by my libido. As much as I've always enjoyed sexy times with you, believe it or not, I don't need you or any man to make myself come. I've got a trusty B.O.B. that can help me with that," I tell him, and can feel my cheeks flush. I don't think I've ever been bold enough to talk about sex toys with him. He knew I had them; hell, he bought me one once, since he was gone from home so much.

"God damn, woman. You can't say shit like that to me and not have me fantasizing about watching you pleasure yourself with said device, or better yet, let me be in control of it and teasing you with it."

"Sorry?" I say, almost as a question, as I give him a shit-eating grin and shrug my shoulders. He laughs, an honest-to-god real laugh. I haven't heard him this carefree in I don't know how long, but it's refreshing and makes me think the man I fell in love with all those years ago is actually making a comeback.

"You're a little cock-tease. You know that?" he says, still laughing so I know he's just teasing me.

"Not on purpose, I promise."

"While I'm not a fan of blue balls—and let me tell you, you're giving me one hell of a case of them tonight—just like when we first started dating, I'd never pressure you into something you're not ready for. Just as you can use your B.O.B. to get yourself off, my left hand works just fine. Not my favorite way to come, but when necessary, I make it work," he says, a smirk on his lips.

"Oh, I'm aware. I've cleaned your shower for years now. I know how often you like to get one off while showering," I tell him, rolling my eyes.

"But the moment you give me the green light to touch you again, prepare yourself, sweetheart, because I will rock your world. Preferably all night, and the entire next day. So, when you're ready, maybe find a sitter for the girls. I want you all to myself with no distractions."

"You're sure confident," I tell him, but know, deep down, he'll make good on his promise.

He winks at me. "You know it."

"Okay, big guy, off you go." I point to the front door. "I need to get to bed—alone," I state, stopping him from interrupting me as I know he wants to do. "So that means that you've got to go home."

Telling Derek to *go home* sounds so foreign coming from my lips. His home used to be *here*, and it's still weird to think this *isn't* his home anymore. At least, not for now.

"Such a ballbuster." He chuckles as he stands and stretches. His t-shirt rides up and shows off a small sliver of his V muscles that usually have me dropping my panties and begging for him with just one look, but not tonight. Tonight, I will be strong and not give in to my wants. "I'll see you tomorrow," he says as he stops in front of me. He drops a kiss to my cheek before heading to the front door. "Think of me when you get yourself off tonight. I can promise you that I'll be thinking of you when I come in the shower."

Then, he walks out the door. I stand there, staring at the door long after it closes. *What the fuck just happened?*

I shake myself from my trance when I hear my phone chime from the kitchen. I stop and lock up the front door, then check to make sure the garage door didn't get left open. I grab my cell off the counter and see a text from Derek.

Derek: If you need me to talk you through that orgasm, feel free to call me once you're between the sheets. I'll gladly listen to you come over the phone.

Jillian: Goodnight, Derek.

Derek: Come on, baby. You know you used to enjoy phone sex before the girls were born. We've talked each other through many orgasms over the years.

He's so cocky and sure of himself, it's almost starting to tick me off just a bit, so I ignore his last text and flip my phone to silent. I grab the remote from the end table and turn off the hockey game he'd been watching. He's been friends with a few of the guys on the team for a while now. I really miss his agent, Madison, who's now married to one of the guys who used to play for the Eagles' hockey team and is now part of their broadcast team. She decided to leave the workforce recently, since they're expecting twins. Derek really spiraled without her guidance, but I get her wanting to be home with her babies. Having two less than two years apart was hard enough; I couldn't imagine having two at once.

I finally make my way to bed and force myself to fall asleep without fantasizing about what Derek's tongue or cock could be doing to me right now. No, I force myself to fall asleep, all alone in this big cold bed.

SEVEN

DEREK

I make it home, still hard as a fucking bat, but on cloud fucking nine knowing I've got a chance at getting Jillian back. I knew she didn't really want the divorce, but I had my head shoved so far up my own ass I couldn't see that until it was all taken from me. Well, I've pulled my head from my ass and I can see clearly. Not being with my family right now fucking sucks, and I've got no one to blame but myself. I don't blame Jillian for doing what she did.

I bypass my kitchen and living room and head straight for the master bathroom. I reach in and turn the water on, giving it a minute or so to warm up while I strip out of my jeans and t-shirt. I toss my baseball cap on the counter, then give my cock a good few tugs before I walk into the shower. The water hits my back and my muscles relax instantly. I plant one palm flat against the shower wall, the other gripping my cock, and I think of all the things I want to do to Jillian's pussy. The way I'd devour it with my mouth. Bring her right to the edge, then pull back, only to bring her right back to the edge a few more times, prolonging her orgasm to make it that much stronger once she does detonate. The way it would feel when I finally slide my cock back inside her tightness. To feel her muscles clench around me. Even after pushing out two kids, she's never not felt like a vise grip latching on to my cock.

I stroke faster, gripping tighter as I work myself from base to tip, making sure to circle around the tip every few strokes. I call out her name as I tumble over the edge and let my orgasm claim my body. My chest is heaving as I coat the wall with my cum. I haven't come that hard in a long-ass time, and I'm a little shocked at how labored I am because of it. I collapse against the wall, making sure to avoid the result of my release sliding down the wall.

Seeing it coating the wall makes me laugh at her comment about being the one to clean the shower I've used for years, and knowing how often I'd rub one out in the shower. I reach up and grab the removable showerhead, then point it at the wall to help wash away the evidence of my orgasm. Satisfied it's all gone, I replace the showerhead and reach for the body wash to actually take a shower.

I slide beneath the sheets, with only a pair of boxers on, after the nice, hot shower. I flip the TV on and watch the highlights from the Eagles game. They've had a rough start to the season, and recently had to start using their back-up goalie, as their main one got injured. I haven't met this new kid, Beckett, yet, but he looks pretty good between the pipes, so I hope they can find their mojo once again. They've been such a powerhouse team the last decade that it's hard to see them struggle this season.

While I might not play their sport, I not only want to cheer on the other local sports teams, but a lot of us players end up at the same charity events or industry parties that span multiple sports, not to mention the number of players from both organizations who use the same agent or agency to represent us. It's nice to have someone local. A lot of my friends have used larger sports agents that are all located in LA and New York City. They can be hard to become acquainted with, and many feel like they're just another number in the agent's column.

When Madison was my agent, she practically knew every breath I took. She did a pretty good job of keeping my ass in line and I sure miss her now that she's off being a mom-to-be and wife. A player, of all people, locked her down. I was never interested in Madison since, by the time I met her, I was already married to Jillian, and never have seen Madison in that kind of light. Today, she and her husband, Richard, are pretty good friends, but she's probably heard by now about the separation and divorce situation.

I'm glad to see the final highlights showing the Eagles pulled off the win, one they desperately needed tonight. I've been in that situation and all it takes is just one win to turn your season around. I click the TV off and force myself to drift off to sleep. I want to text Jillian one last time, but I think I pushed her a little too far earlier. I was trying to be playful, but maybe I didn't go about that the right way. She does that to me, occasionally, but I need to keep that in mind for the future.

I wake up the next morning, ready to start cooking up a game plan to win Jillian back. She gave me the small opening last night and I won't waste it, nor take it for granted. I make a quick protein shake and down it on my way to the gym. Lifting some weights will help me focus and figure out my game plan. It needs to be perfect.

"Hey, man," Jose, one of our outfielders, greets me as I walk into the locker room.

With this being the offseason, many of the guys go back

to wherever they're from, but Indianapolis has truly become home to Jill and me. Once the girls came along, we really started staying put during the few months between seasons. We'd travel to visit family or whatnot, but we stopped packing up our lives for the few months I'd be off and not required to report. But, since we're here, the facilities are all accessible to me as a player.

"How's it going?" I ask, bumping my fist against his.

"Can't complain. Just trying to bulk up a bit before next season."

"Understand that. Are you going back home at all during the break?"

"Yeah," he says, lifting his ball cap off to scratch his head, then sets it back in place. "I'm flying out at the end of the week. My mom wanted me to bring the kids, but Jessica put her foot down that we can't be taking them out of school whenever we want, nor for an undisclosed amount of time. So, it's just me going for a couple weeks, and our compromise was that I'd fly my mom back here for the holidays and then she can see the kids."

"Sounds like a good plan."

"You got anything going on?"

"Trying to convince Jillian to not only take my ass back, but I also sprung the idea of a Disney World trip for the four of us on her for the week after Thanksgiving."

"You don't tread lightly, do you?" he asks, laughing.

"Not really."

I walk over to one of the treadmills and set it up, then jump on it and get a good warmup run knocked out. With my blood pumping hard after ten minutes on the machine, I head for the free weights and start working the muscles. I like to hit all the muscle groups rather than focus on an entire muscle group for a day and nothing else.

I finish up my arms and move on to the leg press, working on my legs. As a pitcher, I not only have to have strong arms to throw the ball at the rate I do, but I also need powerful legs to help give me the power I have to transfer into the ball when I release it from my hand.

With my workout out of the way, I stop in the locker room to shower and change before I leave. I check to make sure I didn't miss any calls or texts while I was working out.

Jillian: Any chance you're free this morning? Penelope woke up with a fever, swollen throat, and has puked. The whole nine yards. I'm suspecting strep, but I need to take her in to the doctor this morning and would prefer to not take Addison with us if you'd be able to stop over and hang out with her, or take her with you today.

The text from Jillian is from about fifteen minutes ago, so I hope she hasn't already had to leave for the doctor.

Derek: I'm on my way. Can I pick up anything on my way for any of you? Coffee? Medicine? Bleach?

The bubbles pop up instantly as I walk out of the building and to my truck. Her text still hasn't come through by the time I'm pulling out of my parking spot, so I toss my cell in the cup holder and hit the button on my dash screen to just call Jillian from my truck's Bluetooth.

"Hey, sorry for bugging you, but I'm in the truck and couldn't read or reply to your text. Did you need me to grab anything before I come over?"

"I think we're good for now. That might change later, but for now, we're good."

"Okay, I'll be there shortly," I tell her before disconnecting the call, and haul ass over to the house.

I let myself into the house from the garage. I still have the opener programmed to my truck. When I first walk in, I'm greeted with complete silence. That doesn't last more than thirty seconds as I hear Pen start to sob as she pukes again. It's obviously freaking her out by the way she's crying. I quickly find them in the master bedroom, Jillian holding a bowl under Penny's chin. I almost lose my protein shake when my own body's gag reflex triggers as I hear and smell her puking. I head for the bathroom to grab a washcloth, getting it wet so Jill can place it on Penny's forehead to help cool her down as her body fights whatever it is that's plaguing it.

"Here, take this," I say quietly, handing over the wet washcloth.

"Thanks." She wipes Penny's face with it as she falls back against the pillows, her little body collapsing into them as her eyes drift shut. From the way they're set up in here, it looks like this has been happening for a while, and it just twists the metaphorical knife to my heart that I wasn't here, yet again, when my family needed me during the night.

"What time is her appointment?" I murmur, not wanting to wake her up.

"Eleven thirty."

"Okay, has Addison had breakfast yet?"

"No, she's still asleep, if you can believe that. Actually, can you go in and check on her, make sure she isn't running a fever? I'm expecting her to come down with whatever this is since they obviously share germs, so it's only a matter of time before that happens," Jillian says, the exhaustion obvious.

"Of course." I grab the thermometer off her nightstand

and head for the girls' room. I find Addison awake and looking at a book while she lays in bed. "Morning, baby girl. Are you feeling okay?" I ask, as I sit down on her mattress.

Rather than answer me, she just shrugs her shoulders. I reach a hand out and feel her forehead. Unfortunately, she's burning up. I don't even need the thermometer to tell me she's got a fever, but I still slide it over her forehead so I can tell Jillian how high it is. "Looks like you've got a fever, just like your sister. Does your stomach or throat hurt?" I ask, and she nods her head.

"My throat," she croaks out.

"Okay, you sit tight, and I'll go get you something to drink and some medicine that will help you feel better."

I stop in the bedroom and relay this information to Jillian. She hands me the kids' ibuprofen and I head for the kitchen to grab a water bottle for Addison to use while in bed. I watch as she chews the tablets and downs some of the water. "Are you hungry at all? I could make you some toast if you feel like eating anything."

"I just want cuddles," she says, obviously not feeling well.

"I'll tell you what. How about we go stretch out on the couch and turn on a movie, and Daddy will cuddle you the entire time. Mommy is in cuddling sissy since she's also sick."

"Okay," she agrees, and I scoop her up in my arms, blankets and all, and carry her out to the living room.

"Do you need to potty before we get settled?"

"Yes," she says, so I bring her to the bathroom. I leave her to do her business and grab a bowl to keep in the living room, just in case she follows in her sister's footsteps and starts to puke. I want to be prepared.

I settle us both in on the couch and flip on the TV, going

right to the Disney Jr. channel, which I know is the girls' favorite one. Addison cuddles into my arms as we lay together, and the heat radiating from her fever is causing me to start sweating. I do my best to uncover my body from her blanket, but it doesn't do much good since she's plastered to me and is burning up.

I nod off for a while with Addison in my arms, only waking up when Jillian shakes me. "I was able to get Addison added to the appointment, since I'm sure they both have strep at this point and will both need antibiotics."

"Okay, still the same time?" I ask, wiping a hand down my face, attempting to wipe the sleep from it.

"Yep, so I need to get them packed up in about fifteen minutes. Is there any chance you can come with us to help me carry one of them in?" she asks hesitantly.

"Of course. I'm all yours for the rest of the day. You just tell me what you need for me to do."

"Thanks, having a second set of hands is necessary when they're both sick like this. I just hope that they don't pass it to either of us."

"Let me go to the bathroom quick, and then I can help you get them loaded up. Do you want to take the truck and I can drive?" I offer. Seeing how tired Jillian is, she probably doesn't need to be driving right now.

"Sure, that'd be great, actually."

I grab her hand and link our fingers together, squeezing them quickly. "I'm not going anywhere. You can lean on me. We'll get them over this little snafu and having them back to our normal, giggling girls within a few days. I can stay the night to help, if you'd like. I can sleep on the guest bed." Stopping her from protesting, I enunciate the last part once again. "The *guest bedroom*. No funny business going on. I just want to help, and it looks like you need some sleep, so just accept the help, Jillian."

Her shoulders drop as she gives in to my request. "Thanks, Derek. I really appreciate it."

"They're just as much my kids as they are yours. This all shouldn't have to fall on your shoulders. I want to help, so just accept that reality and let's get ready to head to the pediatrician."

EIGHT

JILLIAN

"Your suspicions were spot-on. They both are positive for strep," Dr. Dunn says as she walks back into the exam room we're all in. The girls are both passed out on our laps, after having been examined and then waiting on the test results.

"Hopefully it passes quickly then," I state.

"It should. I've already sent the antibiotics for both of them to the pharmacy on file. If either of you start feeling sick within the next seventy-two hours, I'd suggest being seen for a course of your own antibiotics. Both girls will be contagious for the next day or so, but should start to feel better once they've got a day's worth of meds in them. As for the other symptoms, just treat as needed. You can continue to rotate the children's Tylenol and ibuprofen, as needed, for fever or any headaches and-or body aches they may have."

"Thank you," Derek speaks up before I can.

"Your girls will be back to their normal giggly, twirling selves within the next day or two. In the meantime, just keep up on hydration and meds, as needed. Don't hesitate to call us if you need anything, or if they don't start to respond to the antibiotics within the next forty-eight hours."

"Thanks, Dr. Dunn." We follow her out, each carrying a sleeping child in our arms.

"Yeesh!" I say a few minutes later, finally setting Penelope down in her car seat. I shake my arms out, helping to return blood flow properly to them. "She's getting heavy, especially when it's all dead weight."

"They both are," Derek agrees as he gets Addison settled in her seat. We finish up with securing both girls, then climb into our seats. "I figured I'd swing into the pharmacy on the way back to the house. Do you want me to just go through the drive through, or do you need anything else? Are you stocked up on the kids Tylenol and ibuprofen?"

"It wouldn't hurt to pick up both. My luck, we'd run out at two a.m."

He winks at me as he pulls out of the parking lot. "Wouldn't want that, now would we?"

It only takes us a few minutes to drive to the pharmacy. Derek pulls into a spot and hops out of the truck. "Need anything else?" he asks, holding his door open.

"Maybe some mini cans of Sprite or 7-Up, as well as a box of Pedialyte popsicles."

"Anything else?"

"That's all I can think of for now," I tell him and he shuts his door. I watch as he walks inside and out of my view, then pull my phone from my purse to pass the time. Both girls are still asleep in their car seats. I scroll through my Facebook feed, then flip over and do the same on Instagram. I snap a picture of the girls sleeping and post it on a whim. It doesn't take long before my phone pings with a text message.

Mariah: What's wrong with the girls? Why didn't you tell me they were sick?

Jillian: They're both down with strep. It hit them hard and fast. We just left the doctor about ten minutes ago. I'm sitting outside the pharmacy right now.

Mariah: And is that the inside of Derek's truck?

Jillian: Why yes, it is.

Mariah: Ugh, strep sucks. Sorry they're both down with it. And why might you be in his truck?

Jillian: Because I called him to come stay with Addison. Penny was the first one down. She was sick all night. It wasn't until this morning that Addy got sick. Since he was already at the house, I asked him if he could just come to help me with the girls at the appointment. It was a good thing since they both passed out and had to be carried out to the truck. He's inside now, grabbing their meds and a few things to get us through the next day or so.

Mariah: Well, I'm glad to hear he's stepping up and helping.

Jillian: He's been really great, actually. Only time will tell if it continues.

Mariah: And do you want it to continue?

Jillian: Of course, I do. I've always wanted Derek more present and involved.

Mariah: You can be honest; you just want to get laid again.

Jillian: Well, you're not wrong. And he is talented in the bedroom....

Mariah: Lalalalala.... please. No details. :puking face:

Jillian: You were the one to bring it up.

Mariah: I'm sorry. I won't do it again.

Jillian: Why don't I believe you?

Mariah: Call me if you need anything.

Jillian: Nice subject change. I'll let you know. Thanks.

I slip my phone back into my purse, then lay my head back on the seat and close my eyes. I relax into it, listening to the radio quietly playing in the background. The exhaustion starts to set in, and I drift off to sleep as we wait. I pop awake when Derek opens the door, the noise causing me to startle.

"Sorry, I didn't mean to wake you," he says quietly as he settles into his seat.

"It's okay. Did you get everything?" I ask, looking at the bags he's got in his hand.

"I think so. Antibiotics, ibuprofen and Tylenol, some 7-Up and Pedialyte popsicles, and last but not least, a bottle of wine for you," he says, a small smile on his face.

"You really thought of everything," I tell him as I take the bags from him. He buckles up, then pulls out of the parking spot. I relax back as he drives us home.

THE GIRLS ARE SETTLED IN THEIR BEDS, BOTH medicated and sleeping off respective fevers. I check on each of them once again, making sure their temperatures are coming down after the last dose of Tylenol. I quickly scan their foreheads with the thermometer and find that both are coming down, albeit slowly. I sneak back out of their rooms, not wanting to wake them, then head for the living room to relax.

"I was going to order us some takeout. Do you want anything specific?" Derek asks as I enter.

"I'm not picky tonight." I take a seat at the opposite end of the couch from him. I pull the throw blanket that's laying over the back onto me, the exhaustion hitting me once again, like it did earlier in the truck.

"Why don't you go take a nap? I can wake you when the food gets here, or just put it away and you can eat once you wake up. I'll listen for the girls so you can sleep."

"Are you sure?" I ask as I yawn.

"Positive. Go get some sleep," he reiterates, poking the bottom of my outstretched foot.

"Okay." I stand up, not having the energy to fight about it right now. "Thank you again for all your help today. I really appreciate it," I pause to tell him before I head for my bedroom. I'm really thankful Derek was here today. I don't know how I would have gotten both of the girls to and from the doctor's office with both of them sick.

I stop in the bathroom to brush my teeth and wash my face before changing into some sleep pants and a t-shirt. I'm sure one or both of the girls will be up at some point tonight, seeing as it's only early evening. I slide into bed, pulling the covers up and around me as I slip off to sleep.

I startle awake, looking around as I strain to hear if anyone else is awake in the house. I look at the windows and it's pitch black outside from what I can tell, so I'm sure it's the middle of the night. I can hear faint voices, so I know someone is awake. I blink again, and look at the clock on the nightstand to see it's three thirty in the morning. I can't believe I slept so long.

I slip out of bed, and after a quick pit stop in the bathroom, I quietly make my way out to the living room. I find Derek awake with Penny in his lap. They've got Disney Jr. on quietly in the background, but neither one of them is paying much attention to it as they're talking in-depth about something, or as in-depth as a three-year-old can. My heart melts as I eavesdrop on them. They're talking low enough that I can't quite hear what it is they're saying, not that I really care what it is that has them awake at this hour.

It's moments like these that I miss. The moments I crave for us to have as a family, for the girls and Derek to have together. They're only little once and when these days pass, we can never get them back. I never want him to regret not taking advantage of these moments, and hope he can fulfill his promise of changing and being present more.

"How's it going?" I finally ask, not wanting to be the creeper in the corner.

"We're good. Just having a middle-of-the-night party," Derek says, looking up at me with a big smile on his face.

"That's good. Does that mean that someone is starting to feel a little better?"

"I think so," Derek answers. "This one woke up about two forty-five or so, hungry and with a broken fever. She's had a Pedialyte popsicle and a few animal crackers and has done well with that. I've refilled her water bottle, as well."

"I'm glad to hear you're feeling better, baby girl," I tell Penelope, then sit down next to her and Derek. I press my hand to her forehead and, as he said, her fever is gone. I really hope it's gone for good.

"Did you have a good nap?" Derek asks me a few moments later.

"I did. I crashed quickly and slept like the dead."

"Good. Are you hungry? The food is in the fridge."

Just then, my stomach loudly growls, causing all three of us to laugh. "I'm starving," I tell them between fits of laughter.

"Want me to heat you up a plate?" Derek offers.

I stand up and head for the kitchen. "I can get it. You two look cozy, so stay put."

"Mommy," I hear Penny call out a minute later.

"Yes, baby?" I walk over to the living room entrance and peek in.

"Can I have another popsicle?"

"Sure. Do you want anything to eat?"

"No, just the popsicle," she says, blinking her lashes at me as she gives me that puppy dog "you can't say no to me" face.

"One popsicle, coming right up." I head back to the kitchen and finish making a plate of food for myself, and grab her the popsicle. "Here ya go," I say, handing it over to Derek to help her hold since it's so cold.

"Thank you," she squeaks out between small bites.

"Does that feel good on your throat?" I ask between bites of my own.

"Mmhmmm." She hums as she nods her head.

"Has Addison been up?" I ask Derek.

"She woke up around eleven, for twenty or so minutes. Went to the bathroom, had some water. I gave her a dose of meds and a popsicle, and she went back to sleep."

"I'm sure she'll be up sooner than later then, hungry."

"Probably. Seems we're all kind of on a weird schedule right now."

"That we are. It's been years since I ate Chinese takeout at"—I pause and look at the clock—"four twenty in the morning."

"We've had some good memories, eating cold takeout in the middle of the night," Derek says, leaning over to tap me on the knee. The smirk that fills his lips tells me he's thinking about what else used to fill those late nights from our college and early days together.

"You could say that," I tell him, remembering just the same. How carefree we were all those years ago, before the responsibility that comes with getting older, having kids, a house, and just life in general. It's amazing how far we've come over the years. I never thought we'd be in this position, both still so in love with each other, yet so far apart at the same time. Would I change it if I could? Hell yes, I would. I want what we used to have. The way things used to be. Before the pressure, before the drinking and the partying, and the chaos that spiraled things out of control and brought us to this point in our lives, our marriage.

NINE

DEREK

I sit on the couch with Penelope on my lap, a frozen popsicle in my hand as she munches away on it. Thank God her fever finally broke and she appears to be feeling a little better. Holding her this last little bit, talking to her, just the two of us, makes me realize all I've missed out on the last couple of years. Makes me realize just how bad I fucked up.

"Do you want to head home so you can get some sleep?" Jillian asks, breaking the silence.

"I'm good. I told you I'd stay. I can sleep here later."

"I can take over if you wanted to go in and sleep now."

"I'm good, Jill. There's nowhere else I want to be right now, okay?" I tell her sincerely, looking her dead in the eyes so she can see how genuine my words are in this moment.

"Okay."

"If you wanted to go back in and get some sleep, you can," I offer. "I'm sure both girls will be full of energy today, now they've had a day's worth of meds in them and fevers appear to be breaking."

"I might go get a few more hours. Wake me if you need

anything?" she asks, standing from the couch. She's got her hair pulled up into a messy bun, sleep pants and a t-shirt on, and not a stitch of makeup, yet she still takes my breath away. She's still the most beautiful woman in the world to me.

As she walks past the couch where I'm seated with Penny in my lap, I reach my hand out and snag hers. I lace our fingers together, squeezing quickly a few times to really get her attention.

"What?" she asks, stopping behind the couch.

"I love you. I know I didn't show it enough these last few years, but I never stopped loving you."

"Derek." My name comes out on a sigh.

"It's true," I say, bringing our clasped hands to my mouth. I kiss the back of hers before I release it. "I'll prove it to you, and that's a promise."

She pulls her hand back, then stares at me for a few moments before retreating down the hall. I can tell my words have hit her and maybe, just maybe, are starting to sink in. Starting to give her hope we can get back to where we once were. That I can once again be the man she can lean on and trust to know I'll have her back, to be the backbone she needs to stand strong.

"DADDY, CAN WE MAKE COOKIES?" ADDISON ASKS AFTER lunch.

"I guess so," I tell her, laughing at her and Penny's antics. The doctor wasn't lying when she said they'd probably bounce back by today. Now, if *I* could bounce back that quick on the lack of sleep I'm running on.

"Yay! Can I lick the spoon?" she asks.

"Ummm. We'll see," I reply, not wanting to commit to anything like that for now. "How about we get Mommy to help us? Daddy's not the best baker and I might burn the kitchen down without Mom's help."

I can man the grill, boil some water, and bake a pizza, but that's about the extent of my culinary skills.

"Mommy!" The girls go running and screaming out of the kitchen. "Daddy needs your help!" they yell out to her.

"I'm right here, girls," Jillian calls back as she walks down the hall and into the kitchen, the girls following close behind her. "What do you need help with?"

"We're making cookies!" Addison exclaims, twirling in a circle in front of Jillian.

"You are?!" Jillian asks, eyebrows shooting up and into her hairline as she looks over at me with a huge smile on her face.

"I couldn't tell them no." I hold up my hands and shrug my shoulders in a "what else could I say or do" manner.

"You're going to have to figure that word out one of these days," she teases me.

I groan. "Don't remind me."

"All right, let's show Daddy how it's done." Jillian walks over to the pantry and starts pulling out ingredients, handing the containers to the girls, who place them on the countertop. "Time to wash up," she instructs all of us. We all take turns scrubbing our hands with soap and water, not wanting any of the girls' germs getting into our cookies.

"Okay, what's first?" I ask, looking at my three girls. If I was a cartoon character, I'd probably have heart eyes or a thought bubble above my head filled with all my thoughts about these three.

"First, we preheat the oven, then measure out all the dry ingredients into a bowl." Jillian presses some buttons on the oven, then pulls a bowl from the cabinet and sets it on the counter. Next, she grabs the measuring cups and spoons from a drawer and places them out in front of the girls. They must already know what to do as they've both pulled up stools and are waiting patiently. "I follow the recipe on the back of the chocolate chip bag, the only thing that I do differently is use a brick of cream cheese to substitute out the eggs."

"Sounds easy enough," I tell her, pulling the bag in front of me to read the ingredients. I grab the one-cup measuring cup, open the flour container, and fill it up, leveling it off and holding it out for one of the girls to take and empty it into the bowl.

"You're good at that," I praise Addison as she dumps the flour, making sure not to make a mess of it.

"Yep!" she agrees with me and I laugh at her confidence.

"Me next, Daddy!" Penny exclaims as I scoop another cup full. I hand it to her once I've leveled it off and she follows suit, just like her sister did, carefully dumping it into the bowl. They take turns with each of the ingredients until we've got everything measured and mixed together.

"Who's ready for a taste?" Jill asks, holding out four spoons.

"Me! Me! Me!" they both yell out, excited to be getting a taste of the batter.

"Okay, go sit down and I'll give you a spoonful." They do exactly that as she scoops a small amount onto two of the spoons and hands them over to each of the girls. "Since we didn't use egg, the batter is safe for Penelope to eat," she tells me as she scoops another spoonful, this one a little bigger, and hands it to me.

"It doesn't taste any different," I reply, licking the spoon clean.

"Nope, yet it allows her to participate, not only while I'm baking, but lets her have a taste of the batter."

"Where'd you learn that trick?"

"One of the food allergy groups I'm in on Facebook. It's amazing what all you can substitute for eggs and not even know the difference. I even like these better once cooked. The cream cheese keeps them soft, even days later."

I watch as Jill gives the batter a few more swipes with the big spoon, making sure the chocolate chips are well mixed in. She then starts scooping it out with an ice-cream looking scoop onto silicone mats.

"Now, we just let them bake, and soon, we'll have warm, melty chocolate chip cookies to have for snack," she says, as she starts to rinse off the dishes.

"Let me do that." I move her aside from the sink. "You sit, take a break," I instruct, leaving no room for argument. I'm a little surprised when she actually does as I say and takes a seat next to the girls at the bar. They've both cleaned off their spoons and I gather them up, placing them in the dishwasher, along with all the other dishes we used for lunch and while baking.

"I was thinking, maybe after cookies, we could all snuggle up in the living room and watch a movie," I tell my girls.

"Elsa!" Penny exclaims.

"Yes, Elsa!" Addison agrees with her.

"I guess that means we're watching *Frozen* then." I glance at Jillian and see the look of shock on her face when she realizes I know what movie the character the girls have mentioned belongs to. "What?" I ask incredulously.

"Since when are you up on your Disney princesses?" she asks, a smirk tugging at the corner of her lips.

"Oh, only for the last what, three years?" I say, thinking back to when Addison would have first started in with them.

"You amaze me sometimes, you know that?"

"Just you wait, I've got lots of amaze left in me," I tell her, giving her a smoldering look. The one I used to give her and *poof*, her panties would drop. The one that told her, her pleasure was my only focus and that I'd rock her world.

Jillian clears her throat and stands just as the timer goes off, alerting us it's time to take the first batch of cookies from the oven. I watch as she expertly removes them, places a new tray in the oven, and then transfers them to a cooling rack before refilling the baking sheet with more dough. Once she's got the tray filled, I step behind her, boxing her in against the counter. My hands are caged around her, setting against the countertop, and I drop my face to her neck, breathing her in. My nose skims along the smoothness of her neck, the one that is perfectly exposed to me since her hair is still pulled up in that messy bun she favors. I place a light kiss just under her ear and watch as the chill runs through her body. She inadvertently presses back against me, my hardness molding to her softness. There's no way she can miss my cock now firmly pressed against her ass and lower back.

"That's right, baby," I murmur in her ear, only loud enough where she can hear my words. "That's all you. If our girls weren't right here in front of us, I'd have you laid out on this counter and would be feasting on you."

"Derek!" she murmurs as I suck her earlobe between my teeth, quickly giving it a gentle tug before I release it and kiss her just below her ear once more.

"Jillian," I state, my voice dropping a few octaves as I practically growl her name.

"We can't do this. Not now."

"When then?" I ask, sliding a hand across her belly and holding her against me as tight as I can.

"I-I don't know," she says between gasps of breath. "I need time. *We* need time."

She pushes back against me. I drop my hand and take a step back, giving her what she's asking for. I want her to know I'll fight for her—us—but I'm also going to give her the space when she needs it. She's in control here and will be setting whatever pace it is that we need to go in order to find our way back to what we used to have, what we used to be.

"Okay," I tell her once we have a little more space between us. I turn her so she's facing me, and cup her face between my hands, forcing her to look up at me. I close the one-step distance, bringing our fronts back together. "You, me, that's all I want. I'll wait however long you need. I love you, Jillian. I need you back. Being here since yesterday has been the best twenty-four hours in my past year and made me realize what all I'd really sacrificed. The three of you are the most important people in my life and I want more of this."

I motion around to the mess of the kitchen, but also the love I can feel between all of us.

"More baking cookies on a lazy afternoon, and rainy or sick days spent on the couch watching movies, and middle of the night conversations. I want it all. The good, the bad, the ugly, the fun and exciting. All of it. I. Want. It. All," I tell her, punctuating the last of it.

I bring my lips to her forehead, not wanting to press my luck by kissing her on the lips. That, and I might not be able to stop myself once our lips lock together. I can feel how much she wants me—us. I just have to wait her out and be there when she's finally ready to say yes to me once again.

"WHAT'S THE PLAN FOR CHRISTMAS NEXT WEEK?" Mariah asks from the other side of the table as she takes a sip of her wine.

"Presents, food. The norm, why?" I ask, draining my own glass of wine. Derek practically pushed me out of the house tonight and told me to go have a good time, that he'd hold down the house. He'd already called Mariah and Tara and made sure they were both free tonight, so we could have a girls' night out.

"Is Derek coming over to the house, or are you guys doing separate things with the girls?" Tara asks.

"He's coming to the house. Spending the night Christmas Eve so that he's there when they wake up on Christmas morning. Then we can keep our traditions alive for the girls," I tell them both.

"Mhmmm... Christmas traditions," Tara says, a smirk filling her lips. "Does that include the naked ones after the kids are in bed the night before?" she adds, bouncing her eyebrows at me.

"Stop!" I laugh at her antics, and have to rub my thighs

together just thinking about it. I've stayed strong so far, these last six or so weeks, since everything has gone down and Derek has flipped a switch. He's stayed true to his word and been at my side anytime I've needed him, and shown up just because he misses us. Even gone out of his way to plan things like tonight for me. "He really has changed. I might be ready to give him a second chance," I tell my best friend and sister.

"Just be careful. That's all we ask. We know you still love him, and it's obvious he still loves you, but just be careful, okay?" Tara says, grabbing my hand and squeezing it.

"Of course. My guard is still up, but he's wearing it down day by day."

"When are you telling the girls about the Disney trip?" Mariah asks.

I convinced Derek to push it off until after Christmas. That way, we could use it as their big gift. We leave the day after Christmas and will be gone for a week and a half. "Christmas morning. It will be the last gift they open."

"I can't wait to see their reactions!" Mariah states. "You should record it!"

"I was planning on it."

"So, did he book multiple rooms, or a suite, or what?" Tara asks.

"We got a suite with three bedrooms. It has a kitchenette, three bathrooms, laundry...basically a small apartment. I've got a grocery delivery already set up to arrive shortly after we do, so that we'll have some snacks and breakfast items in the suite."

"I'm surprised you were able to book that kind of suite with only a few weeks' notice," Mariah chimes in.

"Money talks." I laugh. "That, and Derek might have slipped his name when booking. I've got character meals and fast passes all planned out. It's been fun planning it behind the girls' backs. I ordered some cute shirts off of Etsy that will be here in a few days, for us to wear on different park days. They're going to flip out and I can't wait," I excitedly say.

"I knew the moment you told me Derek brought up going that you'd be all over it." Tara laughs. "Look at you now, matching outfits and planning everything."

"I want them to have so much fun, and the shirts and things will give them something to open on Christmas morning."

"Good luck getting them to go to bed that night. What time are y'all flying out the next morning?" Mariah asks.

"Our flight leaves just after nine, so nothing super horrible. And it's nonstop into Orlando, so by mid-afternoon, we'll be in our suite and ready to head to Downtown Disney for the afternoon, or hit up the pool if the weather is nice enough."

"Sounds like you've got it all figured out," Tara says, just as a server stops back at our table.

"Anyone ready for a refill or can I put in anything else for you ladies?" the young college-aged guy asks.

"I think we're good. Just the check, please."

We've already been here for going on two hours, and all I want to do is take my bra off, pull on some pajamas, and crawl under a blanket with some trashy reality TV on or a book in my hands. I'm crossing my fingers that when I walk into the house, it's quiet and the girls are asleep. Derek promised he'd handle bedtime for me tonight.

I WALK IN FROM THE GARAGE TO A MOSTLY DARK AND quiet house. Thank God the girls are in bed. They'd be little hellions tomorrow if they were up this late at night. I hang my purse on the hook, making sure to drop my keys in it so I don't misplace them, as I've been known to do. I kick off my heels, not really knowing what possessed me to wear them out tonight. As much as I love the look of them, they kill my feet and back when I do. I quietly pad into the kitchen, seeing that Derek cleaned up after feeding the girls dinner: homemade pizza he was going to let them help make. He really has amazed me these last few weeks with how much he's stepping up and turning back into the family man I knew he could be.

"Have a good time?" His deep voice scares me and I yelp out and jump.

"Holy shit, you scared the bejesus out of me," I tell him, my hand smacking against my chest.

"Sorry," he says, and laughs.

"No, you're not." I laugh along with him. "How'd things go around here?" I ask, taking a seat on one of the bar stools.

"Great. The girls loved making the pizzas with me. We might have made a little bit of a mess with the sauce and cheese, but nothing a few paper towels didn't fix. Then, once it was done, I've never seen both of them eat something so fast."

"You should see the kitchen some days after we've been in here experimenting or baking all day. They aren't always clean when they help. But it's worth it to see their little smiles and to hear them laugh. I love it. I'm going to miss Addison so much next year when she's off at kindergarten all day, every day."

"I can't believe our girls are growing up so fast," Derek muses.

"I know, tell me about it."

"So, did you have a good time tonight?"

"I did, thank you for that."

"Anytime. You deserve to have time out with your friends and for yourself. You do so much around here and for the girls, it's the least I can do once in a while. Plus, it gives the girls and me time to have some daddy-daughter time. Speaking of that, do you have any issues with me taking them out Christmas shopping tomorrow for a few hours? We talked tonight, and they both wanted to buy a few presents."

"I don't have any issues with it. Just don't go overboard, please. They're already going to be spoiled with the trip."

"Oh, we won't be buying anything for them. They wanted to pick out something for *you*."

"Now, *that* will be comical. What in the world will a three and four-year-old think Mommy will want?" I muse.

"They had some pretty good ideas when we talked about it this evening. But you'll just have to wait until Christmas morning to find out," he says, winking at me.

"What time were you thinking? I might head out and finish up my last little bit if you're going to have them occupied for a while. I need to finish up their teachers' gifts, as well as some things for my parents."

"You tell me. I can take them out early, or as early as the mall opens. What would that be nine, ten, in the morning?"

"I think they've switched to extended hours at the mall, but can look it up." I pull my phone out of my pocket and search for the mall. "Looks like they open at ten, they are just open later than normal from now until Christmas Eve."

"So, I'll come by and get them after breakfast, or do you want me to take them out for breakfast?"

"After is fine. I can't head out and do my shopping until the stores open, either, so no need to head off super early."

"Okay, I'll be here by nine then. Help get them cleaned up and dressed before we head out. Once we're done, I can just bring them back here, so don't feel rushed. We can just hang out until you get back. Or I can take them to my place, whatever you prefer."

"You can bring them back here, that's fine. I shouldn't be more than a few hours, depending on the crowds."

"Sounds good to me. How about dinner tomorrow night? We can order in or take the girls out. Your choice," he tells me.

"I'm sure we can make dinner happen."

"Let's decide tomorrow. For all you know, you'll still be out shopping come dinnertime."

"I sure hope not. As I said earlier, I don't have that much more to get."

"All right, I'm going to get out of here, let you get to bed. I'll see you in the morning," Derek says, moving in closer to me. He drops a kiss to my cheek before turning and walking out into the garage. I hear the door open, then his truck fire up and back out of the driveway as the door closes. He still has the opener programmed in his truck and for as often as he's been coming over lately to help out, I haven't addressed it with him. I figured it wasn't worth the fight, especially with how much he's been trying lately.

With Derek gone, I head for bed, stopping first to peek in on the girls. Both are sound asleep, their loveys in their arms and special blankets tucked in around them. I quietly sneak in and drop a kiss to each of their cheeks before retreating back out and into my room. I scrub the makeup off my face before brushing my teeth and getting ready for bed. I slip between the sheets and feel the mattress pad heater I turned on when I first entered the room starting to heat up the bed. I hate being cold while sleeping, so that was one of the best things I ever purchased.

I pull my kindle out and dive back into the book I've been attempting to read for the past week. By the time I get into bed lately, I can hardly keep my eyes open most nights, so it's been slow going. I only get a couple more pages read before my eyes start to close, so I save my spot and turn my kindle off for the night, allowing sleep to claim me.

ELEVEN

DEREK

"Good morning!" I call out as I enter the house through the garage. I'm a few minutes later than I'd planned on getting here. "Sorry I'm late, the damn line at Starbucks was longer than I expected," I tell Jillian as I hand her the drink I picked up for her.

"Thanks," she says, a slight blush filling her cheeks.

"You're welcome." I drop a kiss to her cheek before I head off to find the girls.

"Daddy!" they both exclaim as I enter the living room and they see me at the same time. Both come running over to me as I open my arms, dog piling into them as I drop down to my knees.

"Are my princesses ready to go shopping?"

"Shopping!" Penelope shouts right in my ear.

"Go get your shoes on and we'll head out," I say before peppering their cheeks in kisses.

I release both of them and they take off on a run.

"Walk!" I hear Jillian call out as they run and scream past her. "You've got your hands full this morning. They've been up since six bouncing off the walls, excited to be going shopping with you, so all I can say is, good luck."

"Nothing I can't handle," I tell her as she laughs, puffing out my chest. I lift my ball cap off my head, running my fingers through my hair before pulling it back on.

"If you say so, big guy." She taps my chest with her hand and I pin her hand there, closing the distance between us, and lower my head down to hers until my lips are next to her ear.

"I can show you just how big of a guy I am, if you need a refresher," I say, just for her to hear. My cock is hard as a fucking bat in my jeans in seconds, and I press against her side, letting her feel just how big I am at the moment.

"Daddy!" Penny calls out. "Let's go shopping!"

"Duty calls," I say, dropping my forehead to Jillian's shoulder as I blow out a large breath, and will my cock to settle down. Now's not the time for this, and I start rolling through stats, or sweaty balls hanging out in the locker room. Anything to get the blood flowing back throughout my body.

"Have fun," she says, laughing even harder now.

"Enjoy your time alone," I tell her, stepping back as the girls come looking for me.

"Daddy. We've got to go," Addison states so matter-of-fact, her sass showing brightly this morning. I look over at Jillian, who's biting back her laughter at our daughter's antics.

"That sass is all you," I mouth to Jillian. She just shrugs her shoulders at me with a shit-eating grin on her face.

"Let's get loaded up!" I tell the girls as I start heading for the garage.

"Have so much fun with Daddy!" Jillian calls out at our retreating backs.

"Bye, Mommy," both girls call out before the garage door closes.

I get them loaded up and we're off to the mall to tackle picking up a few things for Jillian *from the girls* for Christmas. When the idea hit me to make the gifts be from the girls, I knew my plan would work. At least, I had great faith it would.

Just as we pull out of the driveway, my phone starts ringing over the truck's speakers, my sister's name flashing on the screen. "Hey, Ry, I've got you on speaker in my truck and have the girls with me," I warn, just in case she's calling about anything Christmas-related.

"Hi! How are my girls doing?" she asks, all chipper.

"Good! Daddy's taking us shopping!" Addison calls out, loud enough for Riley to hear.

"Sounds like fun!"

"What's up with you today?" I ask my sister.

"Not much. I'm headed out to the mall myself to finish up my Christmas shopping."

"When do you fly home?" I ask, knowing Riley plans to spend Christmas with our parents in Southern California, where we grew up.

"I fly out on the twenty-second and come home the twenty-seventh. So, just long enough to enjoy my time, defrost some, but not long enough that Mom and Dad drive me nuts."

"The delicate balance of just enough time back home," I say, laughing at the thought. "How's the job going?"

"It's going. Not great, but it pays the bills for now," she says, not really her normal, bubbly self.

"Everything okay?" I ask, concerned something is wrong.

"I'll be fine. I just think life in general is hitting me hard.

I'm nowhere near home, I've got few friends here in Ohio. I've just got a case of home sickness, I think. So, I'm really looking forward to going home for Christmas," she tells me.

"Sorry you're feeling down. You know you're always welcome here anytime you want to make the drive down."

"I know, and I thank you for that."

"I hate to cut our conversation short, but we're pulling into the mall now. Can I call you later, and we can talk more when we don't have two sets of ears listening in?"

"Absolutely. I was mainly just calling to say hi. But do call me back."

"Sure thing, Ry. Love you. Tell Aunt Ry goodbye," I tell the girls, and they happily oblige before we disconnect the call and I shut off my truck. "Ready to do some shopping?"

"Yes!" they both cheer as I climb out of the truck, then help both of them out behind me.

"What do you girls think?" I ask them a half hour or so later, as we stand in the jewelry store, looking at diamond stud earrings. Jillian had wanted a new set for a while, but I never got around to buying her a pair, so that's changing now. The girls ooh and ahh over the sparkly gems in the display case.

"These ones," Addison says, pointing at a large set.

"I'm not sure those are Mommy's style," I tell my daughter, nixing the idea of buying the largest ones they have in the case. Jillian has never been the flashy type. Hell, she'd never agree to allowing me to upgrade her wedding ring because she was too attached to the one I bought to propose to her. The one with a tiny-ass diamond, since that's all I could afford back then. Now, I could probably buy every last piece of jewelry in this store and it still wouldn't make much of a dent in my bank balance.

"How about these?" I point at a better set sitting in the

very center of the display case. One of the sales ladies is finally free and comes over to help us.

"Good morning, can I help you with anything?" she asks, flashing me a flirty smile. I'm sure she's recognized me from the way her eyes grew a little bigger as she takes me in.

"My girls here are buying a pair of earrings for their mom. I think we like these ones," I tell her, pointing at the pair I'd just pointed out to the girls.

"She will just love these," the sales lady coos as she opens the case and pulls them out. "This set is two carats, with white gold. The sales price on this set is six thousand," she adds, before handing over the set for me to look at.

"We'll take them. Can you box them up for us?" I ask, passing the earrings back to her.

"Of course, Mr. Smyth," she says, confirming my suspicions that she recognizes me. Not that that's not normal these days. I just hope my cover isn't blown because she goes blabbing her mouth to a reporter, or snaps a picture with her cell phone to try and sell to the tabloids.

We get through the purchase and are on our way to the next store in the mall. I let the girls pick out some bath bombs in Lush before we make a stop at Bath & Body Works. I know Jillian loves the scented hand soaps they sell, so we go through and the girls once again help me pick out a handful of them for her.

"How about some lunch?" I ask my girls as we leave Bath & Body Works, my hands becoming full of our purchases so far this morning.

"Yes!" both girls squeal as they jump in excitement. I lead them to the large food court in the center of the mall and check out all the options.

"What do you want for lunch?" I ask them, as I'm still scanning the different places.

"Pizza!" Penny calls out.

"Chicken!" Addison says, most likely referring to the Chick-fil-A.

"Of course, you couldn't make this easy on Daddy." I laugh at my girls. "Let's go get in line," I tell them as I lead the way. Thankfully, the pizza place and the Chick-fil-A are side by side, so after going through the line of one, we hop into the other line. Once we've got all our ordered food, I let them lead the way to find a table, where we all dig in.

"Daddy, can we play after we eat?" Penny asks, pointing to a play area they have in the mall just off the food court.

"Maybe for a few minutes, but you need to finish your lunch first," I tell her as I finish off my chicken sandwich.

"Okay," she says, taking another bite of her food.

"Did you both get enough to eat?" I ask them a few minutes later as I start to toss all our trash onto the food tray.

"Yes," they both tell me at the same time.

"Can we go play now?" Addison asks, batting her eyelashes at me.

"In just a second. Help me clean up our trash and I'll come sit over there with you."

They both do as asked, helping me get all our trash picked up and into the trash can. We wander our way through the maze of tables and over to the play area. I find a place where I can sit and watch them as they run and play, blowing off some much-needed energy.

I've already gotten most of the items on my list for Jillian. The last thing I wanted to get her was a new pair of her favorite pajamas, so with a game plan of one last store to go to, I sit back and let the girls play for about another half hour before we head for the last stop on our shopping adventure.

"Did you have fun shopping with Daddy?" I ask the girls as they come running into the kitchen.

"Yes! We bought lots of things that you'll love!" Addison tells me.

"Don't ruin the surprise now!" Derek says to the girls. "Remember, it's a secret what we bought Mommy today. She'll get to open her presents on Christmas morning, just like the rest of us."

"Okay," Addison answers, then runs off to go play.

"Did you get all of your running around done?" he asks me.

"I did. Thank you. Now, I just have to assemble the girls' teachers' gifts and can drop them off at school on Monday when I drop the girls off."

"Do you have everything ready for the big gift?"

"I do. I've even got most of it all wrapped and ready to go for Christmas morning."

"I can't wait to see how they react. Are you going to record it?"

"That's my plan. I know our parents, and everyone will

want to see it, so I figured I better record it so we can show them."

"Sounds good."

We fall into a comfortable conversation as I work on the dishes while Derek sits on the stool across the counter from me. It's nice when we have the time to connect like this. When nothing is being forced, there's no pressure. Just him and me.

It's finally Christmas morning and the girls are up bright and early at five a.m. I stumble into the kitchen and switch the coffeemaker on to get that going, then pull the breakfast casserole out of the fridge and start the oven so it is pre-heated when we're ready for it later.

"Morning," Derek sleepily says as he walks in, looking for a cup of coffee.

"Are you ready for this madness?" I ask him, knowing just how crazy things are about to get.

"I will be once I get that cup of coffee in me," he says, yawning big as he runs his hand through his hair. It's a little longer than he normally keeps it and my fingers itch to run through it.

"I hear ya on that one." I pull a couple mugs down from the cabinet and fill them with hot coffee. I add a splash of creamer to my own. "Creamer?"

"No thanks, black is perfectly fine for me," he says, accepting the mug filled with piping hot coffee.

"Can we open presents yet?" Addison whines from the doorway of the kitchen.

"Give us just a couple more minutes, but I promise you that it will be soon."

"Okay," she says, scampering off.

"I've already got trash bags set out for us to try and keep the mess to a minimum."

"Sounds good. I'm ready when you are," he tells me, holding up his cup of coffee, ready to go let the girls have the time of their life, opening presents.

"I'll follow you," I tell him, topping off my cup before following him into the living room.

"Who's ready to open presents?!" Derek calls out to the delighted squeals coming from two very excited little girls.

"Okay, take a seat and Daddy will hand out a present to everyone," Derek tells them. We all sit around the living room and he does just that, finding something for each of us to open up. The girls each open a new outfit, while Derek opens a travel toiletry bag I ordered for him *from the girls*, and I opened a box filled with soaps from Bath & Body Works.

We continue opening presents, Derek taking control of passing presents out, occasionally handing me one to open, always tagged as being from *the girls*.

It takes us over an hour for the girls to get through everything as they stop to play with things along the way. We finally get to the point when it's time to open their Disney gift, so I step out to get the big box.

"We've got one last present that's for all of us!" I tell them, carrying the box into the living room. I place the box down in the middle, then set my camera up to capture the reveal. "Okay, open!"

We watch as they pull the top off and pull out the Mickey and Minnie Mouse large stuffed animals I picked up. I printed off a large sign, announcing our surprise.

"What does it say?" I ask the girls, knowing they can't read yet.

"Read it!" Addison says, shoving the sign into my hands.

"It says..." I start, and pause dramatically. "We're going to Disney World!"

"Disney!" they both yell excitedly.

"We leave tomorrow morning," I tell them a moment later.

"Tomorrow!" Penelope exclaims.

"Yep, tomorrow! Some of the outfits you opened are for our trip, so later today, you can both help me get your suitcases all packed. All four of us are going together."

"Daddy gets to come?" Addison asks, a little hesitation in her voice. I know they're confused as to what's going on with everything, and I hate that for them, but I also love how things have been going lately. How much he's been involved and present. It's refreshing to see him making an effort to change and stick to his word since the divorce was finalized a few months ago.

"I do! I'm the one that convinced Mommy that we should go," he tells them, flashing me a wink.

"Can we pack now?" Addison asks, bouncing with excitement.

"Maybe in a little bit. I'm going to go get breakfast finished up. I'm starving!" I tell her, tickling her belly.

"St-stop, Mommy!" She giggles as I tickle her a moment longer, then I head into the kitchen.

"Breakfast is ready," I call out about fifteen minutes later. I'd snuck away while the girls were opening presents earlier to put the casserole in the oven, knowing that once we finished opening, everyone would be hungry.

"Smells good in here," Derek states as he stops behind me. His body is close enough I can faintly feel the heat radiating off of him but can't quite feel him, as we're not touching. It wouldn't take much to change that; just a half step or so and I could have my back pressed against his front. It's so tempting, but I stop myself from making that small step back. I miss the intimacy we once had, the feeling of his skin against mine. The way he could so expertly play my body into such immense pleasure. "Need any help?" he asks, his breath on my skin as he talks lightly, directly into my ear.

"N-no," I say, a little breathily. He must notice what his closeness is doing to me because he chuckles under his breath and blows air lightly on my neck. I can feel the skin pucker with goose bumps before his lips touch the place just under my ear he knows drives me crazy.

"Breakfast," the bastard says a moment later. He stands to his full height behind me and reaches around me to grab one of the plates, and then the other to pick up the second kid plate I had already dished up. He carries them to the table and calls for the girls to come sit down and eat. With them settled at the table, he walks back over and grabs their milk cups and the bowl of fruit I'd pulled out of the fridge to place on the table, as well. "You coming to join us?" he turns to ask, a smirk upturning the edges of his very kissable lips.

"Of course." I straighten my back and attempt to change my facial expressions to not give away just how much he's affecting me. How close I am to saying fuck it and jumping him when the girls aren't looking.

I take a seat at the table and do my best to ignore the smirk firmly planted on his face. *The bastard!*

"After breakfast, you can go play with some of your new things," I tell the girls as they eat.

"When can we pack and go to Disney?" Addison asks, the excitement spilling out of her.

"We can pack this afternoon, and we don't leave for the airport until the morning."

"I wish we could leave today," she says, blowing out an exaggerated breath.

"Sorry, baby girl, we can't go until tomorrow," Derek tells her, leaning over and dropping a kiss to the top of her head. "But I promise you that it will be worth the wait."

"Can I meet a princess?" she asks, her excitement back.

"I'm sure that can be arranged." He winks at me, as he knows we've already booked a character meal for one night with all the princesses.

"I can't wait!" she exclaims.

"What about you, Penelope, are you excited?" Derek asks her.

"Minnie Mouse!" she says, with just as much enthusiasm as Addison had about the princesses.

"That's right, you'll get to meet Minnie Mouse," I tell her.

We all finish up eating and the girls race off to go play with their new toys. I clean up from breakfast, and Derek helps, so it goes quickly. With the kitchen cleaned, I top off my coffee cup with the fresh pot I'd set to brew while we were cleaning.

"I'm going to go grab a shower while they're happily playing," I tell him, taking a sip of the hot coffee.

"That's fine. Want company?" he tosses out offhandedly.

"No," I deadpan.

"Oh, come on, you know it would be a good time," he teases.

"Someone's got to watch the girls," I toss back at him. This slight flirtation is nice...weird...easy. I can't quite put my finger on it, but it's something and I'm not sure how I feel about it.

"You wound me," he says, clutching his hands to his chest as if I just shot him.

"Nice try." I smirk as I walk away and toward my room.

I slip under the hot water, allowing the heat from the water to relax my muscles. Knowing the girls are under adult supervision, I can actually take my time showering. When Derek isn't here, I've gotten used to showering in under five minutes. But with him in the house, I savor the moment and let the water relax me. I scrub and shave and prep for the days ahead, knowing wearing shorts again is a possibility.

Once out, I lather myself with my favorite lotion before pulling on a pair of yoga pants and a cozy sweater to keep me warm on this chilly Christmas Day. Once dressed, I take the time to actually blow dry my hair, leaving it down rather than pulling it up into my signature messy bun. I don't have anyone to impress, but I just felt like doing it for me.

An hour or so has passed since I disappeared into my bedroom, but I find the girls just as they were when I snuck off, playing happily in the living room amongst the large piles of new toys and clothes and all the exciting things they received for Christmas. Derek and I were able to keep up with collecting the wrapping paper into the garbage bags as they opened things. Derek is stretched out on the couch, watching something on the TV as he watches over the girls.

"Feel better?" he asks, noticing I'm looking in on everyone.

"Yes, so much better," I tell him honestly. "Felt good to have more than a five-minute shower."

"I still think it could have felt even better if you'd have let me join you," he teases.

I roll my eyes. "You're incorrigible."

"Only for you, babe." He smirks at me once again, then

pats the open space in front of him on the couch. "Come join me."

"If I lay down now, I'd probably fall asleep."

"Sounds good to me," he says nonchalantly, which has me rolling my eyes at him once again.

"I don't think that's a good idea," I tell him honestly.

"Why? Can't resist being pressed up against me?" The cockiness is rolling off him in waves now.

"Oh, I can resist. Do you not remember the first few months after we met?" I ask, taking him back all those years.

"I remember perfectly. Blue balls for weeks." He winces and shudders, exaggerating it for maximum effect.

I burst out laughing at his antics, thus gaining the attention of the girls. "What's funny, Mommy?" Addison asks.

"Just something Daddy reminded me of," I tell her, not needing to explain to our four-year-old what blue balls are. Derek snickers audibly from the couch and I glare at him from where I stand, and his smirk morphs into a full-on shit-eating grin that fills his entire face. His eyes are dancing with excitement as he listens to how I diffuse Addison's question.

I end up taking a seat on the couch—just not in front of Derek as he tried to get me to do. I sit at the opposite end, pulling the throw blanket over me to keep warm. I grab my kindle from the end table and pull up my latest read. With the girls back to playing, I snuggle in and get lost in my book for a good solid hour or so as they play, and Derek goes back to watching his show.

After lunch, I fulfill my promise to the girls and pull out their suitcases. We pack the outfits they opened, along with other things they think they'll need for the trip. Half of it, I take out of their suitcases once they're no longer paying attention to it, as it isn't stuff we'll need while gone. We pack their backpacks to have on the airplane with coloring books and the iPads, so they can watch a movie or play a game while traveling tomorrow.

We make it through dinner and somehow get the girls to bed on time. I wasn't sure they'd go to sleep because of how excited they are about tomorrow, but with how early they were up and neither of them ended up with a nap today, they both crashed hard and fast.

THIRTEEN

DEREK

"Come relax for a little bit," I tell Jillian when she emerges from down the hall, after getting the girls to sleep. I hold out a glass of wine for her as I drink a beer.

"Today was exhausting," she says, collapsing on the couch next to me and accepting the glass of wine.

"It was." I laugh. "You should have taken a nap this afternoon."

"Should have," she says on a yawn. "I don't think I'm going to be much company tonight."

"Before you get too comfortable or head off to bed, I've got one last present for you," I tell her, reaching for the box on the end table nearest to me. I pick up the earring box and hand it over.

"Derek." She says my name on a sigh and rolls her eyes.

"Just open it," I tell her, rolling my eyes right back at her.

She meticulously pulls the ribbon on it, taking the time to untie it before removing the wrapping paper from the box. Once that's off, she opens the lid and audibly gasps when she sees the diamond earrings in the box. "They're beautiful," she says, running a fingertip over the stones and setting.

"I hope you love them and they're what you were wanting."

"They're perfect. I couldn't have picked better myself if I tried."

"Try them on," I suggest, and she pulls them out of the box and puts them on. "They look great on you, like they were made just for you."

"Thank you." She holds up her phone with the camera turned to the selfie mode so she can see them on herself. "You really didn't need to get me anything," she says, putting her phone down.

"I know I didn't *have* to." I take a swig of my beer. "But I wanted to," I tell her honestly.

A comfortable silence falls between us as I return to watching the TV while Jillian relaxes with her kindle, kicked back at the opposite end of the couch from where I am. Our legs are next to each other's. It would be so easy to intertwine them together, but I don't want to push her. I'm playing a long game here as I try and win her back.

"I think I'm going to head for bed. The girls will be up early with excitement, and with flying tomorrow, I want to be well rested. Plus, we need to be leaving here by six thirty." Jillian says.

"I was thinking of heading to bed myself. If I'm not up when you get up, wake me. I'll help with whatever you need me to in the morning."

"Thanks. I've only got to pack last-minute things come morning time. I already plugged in the girls' tablets so they'll be charged for the flight."

"I can help by keeping them out of your way or whatever you end up needing. We'll figure it out in the morning."

"Sounds good. See you in the morning," she says, standing and stretching before turning in for the night. I turn the TV off and make my way to the guest room, opting for a shower tonight to have one less thing to do in the morning before we head out.

I step under the hot water and let it pound into my muscles. My cock stirs as I think of Jillian just down the hall in bed, then to standing in the kitchen with her earlier. I know the effect I still have on her body; hell, the effect she still has on mine. I grip my cock in my hand—the only action it's seen in months now—and start to stroke it from root to tip. I brace one hand on the wall as I let memories flood my mind. Me undressing Jillian. Sucking her clit between my lips. The sounds she'd make just before coming. The sight of her lips around my cock as she'd suck me off. I increase my strokes until I come, my release coating the tile wall as my breathing is labored. *Fuck, I need to get laid.*

I clean up my mess, not wanting to leave that shit for Jillian, then quickly finish up in the shower and head for bed. Knowing the girls will be up early again and we've got a somewhat early flight, I let sleep claim me as I toss and turn in this empty bed. I long for the night I can slide back into the bed down the hall and pull Jillian into my arms again, rock her world and mine, and then drift off to sleep with her tucked against my side.

"Mr. Smyth, thank you for staying with us. The magic bands you were mailed will get you into your suite, as well as activate the elevator to go to your suite's floor. The suites on that floor have access to a concierge's desk that is staffed twenty-four hours a day, so please do not hesitate to reach out to them if we can be of any service to you. No request is too small or large. They are truly there to help anyone in your party. There is also a nightly happy hour served in the lobby of that floor. They serve beer, wine, a few signature cocktails, as well as some heavy appetizers."

"Thank you," I tell the front desk worker as she helps us finish the check-in process.

"Is there anything I can do for you?" she asks, handing my credit card back over to me.

"Not that I can think of, thanks," I reply before stepping back and pushing one of our suitcases toward the elevator with Penelope in my arm, her head on my shoulder. Once we successfully get on an elevator and get it going to our floor, I adjust Penny. I think she's exhausted from the big day yesterday, combined with getting up at five this morning and all the excitement from flying. She's definitely ready for a nap once we reach the room.

"Did you hear everything the front desk lady told me about the amenities?" I ask Jillian as the elevator comes to a stop and the doors open.

"Some, but I read up about the hotel and knew we were booked on a level with the concierge desk."

"This place is amazing," I say, pushing open the door a moment later, and glance over my shoulder at Jillian. "You did good picking it out."

"Thanks," she says, a small smile cresting her lips as she takes in the room and view we have of Magic Kingdom. "We should have a perfect view of the fireworks from our room, if we're ever in here when they go off."

"We'll have to keep that in mind. Didn't you have a grocery order coming today?"

"Yep, it should be here soon. The bell desk might

already have it, actually. The company said they just deliver it to them, and they'll bring it to us. That way, if rooms aren't ready or flights end up delayed, the delivery person isn't stuck with an order they can't deliver."

"Makes sense." Just then, I hear a knock at the door, so I step toward it and open it to find an employee with a cart filled with grocery bags. "Perfect timing," I tell the guy. "We were just discussing this."

"Good afternoon, sir. Do you mind if I come in to unload?"

"Sure, come right in," I reply, then stand aside so he can push the cart into the room. He quickly unloads the groceries Jillian ordered, placing the bags in the kitchenette area for us.

"Well, that was convenient," she says once he leaves.

"It was." I still have a sleeping Penelope in my arms, so I lay her down on one of the beds.

"You tired, Addison?" I ask her as she sits on one of the couches in the living room. "You can take a nap with Daddy."

"Okay," she says, and I know she's exhausted since she's not putting up a fight.

"I guess I'll be taking a nap. You should take one with us," I tell Jillian.

"Maybe in a little bit. I'll put the groceries away and then lay down. I don't want to let them sleep too long, or else they might not want to go to bed tonight on time."

"Want me to set an alarm for an hour or ninety minutes?"

"Sure. That should be fine. I'm sure once we're out and about, they'll perk up and we'll probably be out a little late anyways, so it will make up for the nap."

"You're the boss," I tell her with a salute, then pick

Addison up off the couch and head into one of the bedrooms. I pull the covers back and lay her down on the bed. Kicking my shoes off, I slide in next to her, making sure to set an alarm on my phone, and we both fall asleep within minutes.

I wake up to my alarm ninety minutes later, quickly reaching for my phone and shutting off the blaring noise. The room is dark and silent, so I slip out of bed and head for the living room. Jillian has already set out all the snacks and stocked the fridge as she said she'd do. I grab a bottle of water and an apple from the counter and bite into it as I go in search of her. Both girls were in the room with me and still asleep when I snuck out. I find Jillian in one of the other bedrooms, curled up with her kindle still in her hand, as she sleeps peacefully. She's covered with a throw blanket she must have found in one of the closets. I stand at the doorway, somewhat like a creeper, as I watch her for a few moments.

I walk over to the side of the bed and sit down. I reach out and take the kindle from her hand, flipping the cover closed before I set it on the nightstand next to the bed. Without thinking, I swipe the hair from her face, tucking it behind her ear, then run the backs of my fingers down her cheek. "Jill," I say, just above a whisper. "Babe, it's been an hour and a half," I repeat, a little louder, trying to rouse her awake. I continue to rub her cheek until she stirs. Her eyes pop open, taking me in, before she rolls onto her back and stretches. Seeing her like this, I have the strong urge to bend over and kiss her.

"What time is it?" she asks, her voice a little hoarse from sleeping.

I look at my watch. "About three forty-five."

"Are the girls awake?"

"Not yet. I was able to shut off my alarm before either of them woke up."

"We should probably wake them up soon," she says, yawning again.

"Or, we could let them sleep and have a romp in the sheets," I suggest, bouncing my eyebrows at her.

"Not going to happen. I don't want to be up all night." She hits me in the side with one of the pillows as she laughs.

"Can't blame a guy for trying."

"Something like that." She fakes a huff. "Let me up, I need to pee," she says, pushing on my side so I'll move out of her way. I do as she asks and stand up, but I don't move far, making it so she presses against me as she slides by. I don't miss the slight hitch in her breathing when she does. When, for a split-second, her body is flush against mine.

"Want me to wake the girls?" I ask just as she walks into the bathroom.

"Yes, please," she says, giving me a small smile before the door shuts.

I head back to the kitchen to throw my apple core and empty bottle of water in the trash before I head to wake the girls up. Thankfully, they both do so easily and are in good moods once awake.

I bring them out to the living room just as Jill joins us. "Do you both need a snack?" she asks them, already pulling a few things from the fridge. Both girls nod their heads as they sit at the table, still looking a little sleep drunk.

"After snack time, we can go explore," I tell them as I look to Jillian for clarification.

"Daddy's right. We're going to go down to Downtown Disney for a while. Have some dinner, maybe pick out a souvenir or two," Jillian tells the girls.

"Will the princesses be there?" Addison asks.

"I don't think so, sweetheart." She sets a plate in front of each of the girls with a half of a cut up apple and some cut up cheese. "But we'll get to meet them throughout our stay! We even get to have dinner with them one night."

"Really?!" Addison perks up and Penelope follows suit.

"Yep. It will be so exciting! You'll get to get all dressed up beforehand, put on your favorite princess dress, have your hair done, and then we'll go have dinner! How does all that sound?" she asks, just as excited as our girls are now.

They both bounce in their seats as they quickly eat their snacks.

"Everyone ready to go?" I ask about ten minutes later, after we've all had the chance to eat, use the restroom, and put shoes back on.

"Yep!" the girls call out.

"We need to stop at the bell desk before we take the shuttle over to Downtown Disney. The rental company delivered the stroller to them about an hour ago, according to the text message I got."

"Sounds easy enough. Anything else we need to do?"

"Nope," she says, slinging a backpack on her back.

"Want me to take that for you?"

"I've got it," she says, grabbing Penny's hand as she opens the door. "Let's go, fam!"

My girls all skip out of the door, and a smile breaks out on my face. I know it was just an easy thing to call all of us, but the fact Jillian still thinks of us as one family makes me hope that one day we'll be back to a solid unit. One that I'll never mess up enough to lose again.

I pull the door shut behind us and follow my three girls down the hall to the elevator. Penny pushes the button to summon the elevator, and once we're inside, Addison presses the button for the ground floor, where we make our way over to the bell desk and collect the stroller. The young man helping us directs us to the shuttle stop that will take us to where we want to go.

The girls excitedly bounce around as we take in everything while we walk through all the shops. We spend lots of time in each one as they look through everything, trying to decide what they can't live without. Jillian helps them both pick out their ears and we have their names embroidered on them. Since that takes awhile, they offer to have them delivered to our room later tonight and we take them up on that service. We also leave the store with a new set of princess pajamas for both of them, as well as t-shirts for them to wear sometime soon.

After time at the shops, we're finally all hungry enough and find a restaurant for some dinner.

"What's the plan after dinner?" I ask Jillian as we all dig in to the appetizers.

"I didn't plan much for tonight, wanting it to be just an easy evening. We can walk around a little more, maybe get some d-e-s-s-e-r-t," she says, spelling out the word, so the girls don't know what she's telling me. "After a little bit, if they're still in good moods, and then call it a somewhat early night and head back for the hotel. I wanted to be at the park in the morning for rope drop, so we need to be up and at breakfast by seven."

"Sounds good." I take a drink of my beer. "It's already seven thirty. I imagine it will be after eight by the time we get out of here, but I'm up for whatever you want to do." Our server arrives just then with our main meals.

We're nearly finished eating when a woman approaches the table, her tits spilling out of her top, and the amount of makeup she's got caked on is comical, at best. Just as she stops next to me, she adjusts her shirt, causing her tits to pop out just a little bit more. I know what's coming and my stomach turns at the thought of it. "Hi Derek," she purrs, and I look directly at Jillian. "Can you sign something for me?"

"I'd love to, but as you can see, I'm on vacation with my family. You can contact my management team and they'll get you all set," I tell her curtly. I don't need this shit right now. Not in front of my girls.

"I thought you were single," she states, not getting the hint I don't want what she's offering.

"My marital status is irrelevant at the moment. I'm with my family and now is not the time," I reply, a little more firmly this time. I see our server, along with the manager, approach our table, obviously having taken notice of what's going on.

"Mr. Smyth, Mrs. Smyth, I'd like to thank you for joining us tonight and I'm extremely sorry for the interruption." The manager glares at the woman beside me. "I assure you, we will escort this woman out and make sure your family can finish up and leave without any further issues," he tells me as I see a security guard approaching our table. The woman makes a fuss as they remove her, but good riddance. I usually don't mind signing stuff for people, especially kids, but not when overzealous fans, especially women, try and shove their chests in my face, thinking that will get them somewhere with me.

"Thank you for that," I tell him.

"Is there anything else we can do for you?" he asks nervously.

"Not at all, everything has been great. And please don't worry. Unfortunately, we're used to these types of fans occasionally interrupting our family time. Thank you for moving in quickly and taking care of the issue."

"Absolutely. We strive to provide the best service to all visitors. We want everyone to have a magical time."

"I think the only thing we need is the check," I tell him before he leaves the table.

"Of course. I think your server was already getting that, but I'll make sure she is."

"Well, that was fun," Jill says, a smirk on her lips as he steps away. Her easygoing attitude has me relaxing just a bit. I was worried she'd be pissed about the intrusion.

"I'm surprised they stepped in so quickly."

"I'm not. Our server was coming by when she first approached you, and I think she realized what was about to go down before it even really started. She quickly did an about-face and went to find the manager and alert security right away. Next thing I knew, they were both approaching, and the rest is history."

I finish off the last little bit of my beer. "She deserves a large tip then."

"I'm sure she wouldn't be opposed to that," Jillian agrees as she helps Penelope wipe her hands off.

"I need to potty," Addison says.

"Me too!" Penelope exclaims, jumping up from her seat.

"All right, let's go to the potty," Jillian tells both of them as she stands.

"Do you want me to wait here for you or out by the entrance?"

"If you're done with the check and we're not back, you can head out to the entrance. If not, then we'll come back here. How's that sound?"

"Sounds good."

She takes off for the bathroom with the girls and I watch as she walks away. Her hips swinging side to side has my dick stirring in my jeans. I watch until she disappears around the corner and down a hallway.

"Your check, sir. Was there anything else I can get for you?"

"No, and thank you for your help," I tell the young server as I hand over the check with my credit card.

"My pleasure. We hate for our customers to be bothered. It shouldn't matter who you are, you should be able to enjoy your dinner with your family without being bothered."

"Thanks, some people don't think the same way you do," I say on a chuckle. "Do you have any kids? Any baseball fans?"

"My nephew is a big fan," she says, a smile on her lips. "He's always running around with a ball and glove in his hand."

"That's great. What's his name?"

"Elijah."

"And how old is he?"

"Five. He'll be six in just a couple weeks."

"Do you have an email address?" I ask. "I'd love to send him something for his birthday, but don't have anything special with me that I can sign. But my manager can send out an entire package."

"That's so kind of you! Are you sure?"

"Positive." I pull my phone out and open up a blank email. "Just type out your email address for me and I'll email it to my manager to contact you to get a mailing address and jersey size. I'll have him send a package. Hopefully we can get it to you before his birthday."

"He's going to flip and I'm officially going to become his favorite person," she says, beaming at me as she hands my phone back.

"I'm glad I can help!" I tell her, typing off a quick message, then sending it.

"Let me go get your card ran and I'll be right back," she says before walking away.

I scroll through some emails while I wait for the server to return with my card and the receipt for me to sign, but nothing really important catches my eye by the time she returns. I sign the slip, adding a normal tip. I slide my card back into my wallet and pull out a few hundred-dollar bills to add to it. I don't necessarily want her to have to wait for the tip to be paid out on her paycheck, so figure cash would be best. I hold off leaving the table, wanting to hand her the receipt book, so I know she gets the tip.

"This is for you. Thank you again for everything. My manager will be in touch very soon."

"Thank you, enjoy your stay."

"Thanks, I have a feeling we will," I tell her before walking off toward the entrance.

I don't have to wait more than a minute before Jillian and the girls join me. Our daughters climb up into the stroller and we take off to walk around for a while longer.

We walk around, taking in the sights and stores all around us. The girls have mellowed out compared to how excited they were before dinner.

"Who's ready for some dessert?" I ask as we approach Goofy's Candy Company.

"Me!" they say in unison, perking up as they look inside the store.

"All right, how about we pick out something and then after we eat our treats, we'll head back to the hotel for bed. We've got a big day tomorrow!"

They both quickly agree, and we make our way inside. We all look over the many delicious-looking options. The girls each settle on Mickey-shaped cookies, while Derek got a huge milkshake, and a fancy decorated candy apple for me.

"How were your cookies?" I ask the girls as they both finish up.

"Yummy!" Addison says. "Can I have another one?"

"Not right now, sweetie. I'm sure you can have one at another time while we're here."

"Okay," she says, attempting to pout.

"Be careful," Derek tells her, reaching in to tickle her belly. "The tickle monster might come get you to turn that frown upside down." His hand connects with her belly and she starts to belly laugh. He pulls her into his lap. "That's my girl!"

"Da-daddy!" She giggles.

"Shall we start heading toward the shuttle?" I suggest a few moments later. We've all finished up our desserts and I've tossed out the trash.

"Mommy says it's time to go, and she's the boss," Derek tells the girls. "Hop in and I'll give you both a ride."

"WELL, THAT WENT A WHOLE LOT FASTER AND EASIER than I thought it would," Derek says, handing me a glass of wine as he takes a seat on the couch.

"They were exhausted, and I promised them we'd see the princesses tomorrow."

"I'm exhausted," he muses as his head hits the pillow behind him. "Even with that nap from earlier."

"Yep," I agree. "Look at us. Not even in our thirties yet and we think ten p.m. is late."

"Life sure does sneak up on you. I can remember the days when we'd barely be leaving to go out for the night."

"Those sure were the days," I reply, thinking back to our college days.

"They sure were. No real responsibilities, or at least not like the ones that we have now."

"Yeah." I sigh before I take a large swallow of my wine.

"I wouldn't change where life has brought us. Well, actually, if I could go back, I'd change a few things, but not you, not our girls. You're the three best things to ever happen to me," he tells me, sitting up and looking me straight in the eyes. "I need you to know that and believe it down to your soul, Jillian."

"I know," I reply, allowing him to link our hands together after he sets my glass of wine down on the table next to us.

"I love you. A day hasn't gone by since we met in college that you haven't held my heart in your hands," he says, pouring his heart out to me. He tugs me to the edge of the chair I'm sitting in, my legs sliding between his, only stopping once our foreheads are resting against each other's. He stares into my eyes for what feels like forever, but in reality, is probably just a minute or two. His lips ghost over my own, tempting me to take things further. He keeps things light, wanting me to make that move. But I hesitate, and he pulls back and gives me a sad look. "What time are we headed out in the morning again?"

"I'd like to be leaving by seven thirty, at the latest. I promised the girls we'd be there for rope drop."

"Okay. What time do you plan to get up?"

"My alarm will be set for six, but don't feel like you have to be up that early. I plan on waking the girls up around six forty-five or so, unless they wake up on their own earlier than that. I already have their outfits ready, so we just need to get them up, feed them, dress them, and we can head out."

"Sounds good, I'll be up by six thirty then."

"Thank you."

"See you in the morning." Derek stands and walks towards his bedroom. He pauses at the doorway and looks back at me. "I'm not giving up and I'll be right here when you're ready again."

He disappears into the room, shutting the door behind him but not latching it fully. I sit back in my chair and blow out a deep breath. My mind is racing with everything. The what ifs. The hurt and loneliness I felt over the past two years. His excessive partying and drinking really took its toll on me and I don't know if I can ever go back to that again. I force myself to stand up and head for the bedroom next to the girls' room. I walk into the bathroom and do my night-time routine before sliding between the sheets of the queen bed, where I stare at the ceiling for what feels like forever. A montage of memories dating back to when we first met in college, cheering him on as he quickly made his way up through AAA ball, and finally being called up to the majors. Celebrating his first trip to the All-Star game. His first post-season game, first division championship, and the subse-quent loss of winning the pennant. Our engagement, wedding, the birth of both girls. We've had a lot to celebrate in the six years we were married, and it just kills me it ended. I still love Derek with my entire being. But can I let the past stay in the past and believe he's changed?

I finally fall asleep, the question rolling around in my mind and causing me to toss and turn all night. I wake up multiple times, as my mind doesn't want to shut down and rest. He's been so attentive the past couple of months, trying to prove to me he's changed, and I want to believe him, I really do.

My alarm goes off and I reach for the nightstand to turn it off. My sleep was so fitful, it feels like I just closed my eyes. I drag myself from bed and head for the shower. Hope-fully between it and coffee, I'll be able to function this morning.

I take a little longer than I'd planned to get showered and dressed, but am pleasantly surprised when I come out of my room and find Derek and the girls sitting at the table, all eating breakfast. The room smells of waffles and coffee. I make a beeline for the pot, filling my travel cup I left out last night. That first sip sends a jolt of caffeine through my body and I almost instantly feel my body perk up.

"Mornin'," Derek's gritty morning voice calls out and I turn to face them.

"Morning," I say before taking another sip of my hot coffee.

"Rough night?" He cocks an eyebrow up at me.

"Yeah, I had a hard time sleeping last night. Tossed and turned all night."

"Sorry to hear that."

"Yeah, not the ideal night for it to happen. I have a feeling I'll be surviving on a lot of coffee today."

"Speaking of coffee, did I make it how you like it?" he asks, lifting his own cup to his mouth. I watch as his Adam's apple works in his throat, forgetting just how sexy that part of a man's body can be. I shake my head a bit, attempting to remove the cobwebs from my mind.

"It's perfect," I finally remember to answer him.

"Want some breakfast?"

"I'm good. I'll just eat a yogurt and grab something else in a little while, once we're at the park."

"Sounds good. Are you girls ready to get dressed?" Derek asks them.

"Yes!" they both exclaim, then get off their chairs and head for the bedroom.

"Where are the outfits for today? I can work on getting them dressed and ready to go," he says.

"Suitcase in their room, outfits are in Ziplocs labeled with name and day. Can you also get their teeth brushing done?"

"No problem," he says and takes off after the girls. I sip my coffee for a few more minutes, then grab the yogurt and scarf it down before I finish getting ready for the day.

EXHAUSTED, I COLLAPSE ON THE COUCH AFTER ONE hell of a long day. I loved getting to experience today through the eyes of Addison and Penelope. Seeing their faces light up with each character we met was priceless. They are going to flip their shit when we have dinner tomorrow night in the castle with all the princesses.

"Wine?" Derek asks and I peel my eyes open.

"A small glass would be nice," I tell him, and he grabs a glass and the open bottle from the fridge. I watch as he pours a few ounces into the glass, then hands it over to me. "Today went well."

"It did. I can't believe they lasted so long."

"The stroller sure helped."

"Yeah, I couldn't imagine making them walk as much as we did today." I look at my watch. "My step counter says we did almost thirty-K! No wonder I'm exhausted, and my feet are killing me."

"Turn this way," he says, sitting down at the other end of the couch. I do as he asks, and he places my feet in his lap, then starts massaging them.

"Ugh...that feels amazing." I moan as he digs in to the arch of my left foot.

My head falls back on the couch armrest as I relax. Between the wine and Derek's hands, I'm going to be a puddle before I know it. A silence falls between the two of us and my eyes close. I crack them open when he switches to my right foot, digging his thumbs into the arch just as he did with the left.

"You're going to spoil me if you continue."

"And what's wrong with that?" He gives me a smoldering look. It would be so easy in this moment to say fuck it, throw caution to the wind, and slide onto his lap. Pull my top off and let him have his way with me. God, what I wouldn't do for an orgasm right about now, that I didn't have to give myself. "If you don't stop staring at my dick in my jeans, I can't be held responsible for it coming out then," he oh so cockily says to me, a smirk pulling at the corners of his lips.

"I wasn't staring at your dick," I lie, and he damn well knows it.

"That's not what the look on your face, nor the blush covering your cheeks, says." He smirks yet again. His thumbs press hard into my foot as he works the muscles over.

"Don't be an ass."

"I'd like to smack your ass," he says, a full-on shit-eating grin now filling his face. I just roll my eyes at him, causing him to laugh even harder. "You know I could make you feel good. Fall asleep nice and orgasm sated."

That smolder—the one that, at one point in our relationship, would have me handing over my panties faster than he could blink—is out in full force, but I've somehow found a way to not react to it. Well, at least not in the way he's used to me reacting to it.

I pull my feet from his hands and stand abruptly. "I'm going to go to bed. I'll see you in the morning," I tell him and escape into my bedroom. I shut the door behind me and then lean against it, sucking in a deep breath. I rest a hand against my chest, willing my heart rate to slow and my breathing to return to normal.

It takes a few minutes, and I stay at the door, listening to Derek moving around in the other room. I can hear the clink of the wine glass I'd used being placed in the sink. I can hear him as he shuffles around, and finally the *click* of his own door closing. I move away from the door and into the bathroom. I first take in my reflection in the mirror and he wasn't joking when he said my cheeks were covered in a blush. Not only are my cheeks, but my neck and chest, as well.

I reach in and turn the water on in the shower, filling the time while I allow it to warm up to brush my teeth. With that done, I strip from my clothes and slip into the shower and under the hot water. I turn it up to the hottest setting I can handle and let the powerful water massage into my tired muscles. Now that the excitement of our first day is over, I'm going to let the girls sleep in tomorrow and we can head over to the park once we're all up and ready. No need to start our day off with cranky kids or adults. I kind of wish I'd thought to invite mine or Derek's parents to come along. While we can easily handle the two of them ourselves, having some extra adults around would be nice.

I finally finish up my shower, my skin nice and pruned by this point. Once dried off, I slip into some pajamas and head out into the kitchen to grab a bottle of water. With that in hand, I turn to head back to my room, but stop dead in my tracks when I see Derek standing a few feet away from me, clad in only his *tight* black boxer briefs. The ones that do *absolutely nothing* to hide his hard cock. My eyes track up and down his body, taking in all the rigid muscles he's worked damn hard to keep over the years.

I'm so lost in my perusal of his body; I don't even realize

he's closing the distance between the two of us until he's inches in front of me. One of his large hands comes up to cup my cheek, while the other slides around my waist, pulling me closer to him and then resting on my ass. The very ass that's hardly covered by my panties and sleep shorts. His lips land against the skin on my neck and he sucks it ever so lightly, driving my want and desire for him up even more, and my willpower to stop this between us falters ever-so-slightly.

"Baby," he rasps in my ear before grazing his teeth over it. "Let me make you feel good."

I don't respond, I just melt against his touch. I absorb it all. The endorphins that are already running through my body have me ready to explode, and he's only touched my neck.

Derek takes control, backing me up against the wall. He cups my ass with both hands and lifts me up, wrapping my legs around his waist, and pins me to the wall with his body. His lips map from my ear to the hollow of my collarbone and back up the other side. His *very* hard cock does wicked things as he presses against my center.

"Fuuuuuck, Jillian," he moans before capturing my lips with his own. His kiss is frantic and punishing. My lips already feel bruised. My control snaps and I give it right back to him. My fingers find their way into his hair, and my hips buck, causing the best friction directly on my clit. The few layers of fabric between us provide not only a much-needed barrier between the two of us, but also an extra sensation as it rubs against my extra-sensitive parts.

"I'm going to come," I whisper against his lips when we break apart for air.

"Yes." He pants and continues to thrust against me. "Come for me, baby," he murmurs in my ear and I do just that. I fall apart in his arms, pinned to the wall of our shared hotel suite. My head rolls back, smacking the wall, before falling forward until my forehead rests against his shoulder.

"What did we just do?" I whisper against his skin and he chuckles at me.

"*We* just came in our pants like two horny teenagers," he says, and it's then I realize I can feel a lot of wetness between my legs.

"You...you came?" I squeak, popping up to look at him.

"Like a fucking fifteen-year-old the first time he sees a pair of tits." He laughs. "It's what happens when it's been so long since I've touched you. My hand only provides so much relief."

"Y-your hand?" I question. I never worried Derek would cheat on me when we were together, but I never expected him to become celibate after we divorced. I know he could have his choice of any woman—hell, last night was proof of that—but I'm blown away he hasn't been with anyone at all.

"There's been no one?" I question.

"Nope," he affirms, popping the P for emphasis. "I told you that I'd be coming for you. Why would I fuck that opportunity up by fucking some random chick? I only have eyes for you, Jillian." He pushes a lock of my hair from my face and behind my ear before cupping my cheek.

"I-I don't know. I just... I don't know what I thought. I just never expected you to be a saint. It wouldn't have been cheating."

"Have you been with someone else?" he questions, and I can tell it pains him to do so.

"No! God, no." Derek was my first, and the thought of just sleeping with a random person "just because" isn't high on my list of things I want to do right now.

"Then we're on the same page. You need some sexual release, you come to me. If I need some sexual release, I'll come to you or fall back on the ole hand."

"It's not that simple, Derek."

"But it can be. You know we're good together. I've already expressed my intentions going forward. Go on a date with me."

"A date?" I question.

"Yes. You. Me. Let me show you that I've changed. Let me show you that it can be like it was in the beginning."

I blow out a large breath, mulling over his suggestion. "Okay," I tell him, and his face lights up.

"You won't regret it," he says before dropping a chaste kiss to my lips. He shifts so I'm no longer pinned and lowers me to the floor. We both look down at the mess we made from our tryst against the wall, and he smirks. "I'm going to go get cleaned up."

"Sorry about that."

"I'm not. I'll gladly do it again." He bounces his eyebrows at me, and I fall into a fit of giggles. "Goodnight, Jillian," he says a moment later as he walks toward his room.

I stay standing in the spot he left me, biting my lip, wondering what in the hell just happened. What did I just get myself into by agreeing to go on a date with him?

I hear the water in his bathroom turn on. Oh no, I can't think of him *naked* and under the water for too long, or I might lose all control and *join* him in the shower. So, I force my feet to move and head toward my own room. I change my sleep shorts and panties, since we made a mess of the ones I have on.

I slip into bed, sated as he said I would be, and maybe just a tad bit excited about the date he's going to take me on in the near future.

FIFTEEN

DEREK

Since the moment Jillian said yes to a date, to another chance at us, my mind has been reeling on what I can plan for said date. I don't really want to wait until we get home, so I set into place some elaborate plans, but ones I hope pay off in the end.

The next few days fly by, between rides and princess appointments and more character meetings than I can count. Today is a down day and we're just spending it at the pool. What Jillian and the girls don't know is that my parents are flying in to join us for the last few days of our vacation. I decided the date couldn't wait until we got home. I needed to go big, and this will hopefully make Jillian realize I'm all-in.

"Daddy!" Penny calls from the side of the pool. "Catch me!" she adds before jumping in, and I do as she asks. The girl has zero fear when it comes to the pool. Thankfully, for three years old, she's a pretty good swimmer due to all the lessons Jillian has had the girls in since they were infants.

"How about we go down the slide?" I suggest to both of them.

"Yay!" they cheer as they cling to me. I walk us out of the pool, thanks to the zero-entry end, and around to the entrance to the slide. I grab a tube for all of us to ride on and we climb the stairs to the top.

"Mommy!" Addison calls down to Jillian. "Watch us!" she shouts, and Jillian gives us a thumbs up. It's finally our turn and I get the girls situated on the tube, then wait for the signal we can go down. My ears are filled with the giggles from both of them as we zoom down the slide. This particular one dumps us into a lazy river, so once we make it to the end, we relax as we make our way around.

"Are you girls ready for some lunch?" I ask as we approach the exit to the river.

"Yep!" they both tell me at the same time.

"Good, because Daddy is starving!" I tell them, moving in to pretend to eat their bellies.

I pull away when it's time for me to steer us to the exit. With the girls out of the water, I toss the tube into the corral and we take off to find Jillian. She's still kicked back in her lounge chair, a fruity drink next to her and her kindle out.

"Hey, Momma. We're ready for some lunch, what do you say?"

"Sounds good to me," she says. "We can flag down our server and order."

We rented a cabana for the day to give us a tiny bit of privacy, and to give us a place to have some shade when needed. Besides the first night at the restaurant, we haven't had any other issues with fans bothering us. I've signed a few things for some kids who recognized me, and taken a handful of pictures, but nothing too bothersome.

"I have a surprise for the three of you," I tell my girls after we've finished our lunch. Jillian's eyebrows raise in question at me.

"Tell us!" the girls both chime in. This week has been chock-full of nothing but surprises for them each day with the events Jillian has planned for this trip.

"It will be arriving at the hotel later this afternoon, probably about four o'clock."

"And what is it that's being delivered?" Jillian asks.

"You'll find that out later," I tell her, and she rolls her eyes at me.

"So, you're just going to drop that little tease on us and not give us anything else?" she quips.

I smirk. "Yep."

"Daddy, that's not nice," Addison says, her little hands going to her hips as she gives me a look that could kill. I can't help it, but I bust out laughing at her little sassy attitude. She's going to be one hell of a handful in ten years.

"That's right. You tell him, Addison," Jill tells her.

"Okay, one hint. Someone is coming to spend the rest of our vacation with us," I reply. "But that's all you get until they arrive."

Jill gives me a shocked look, one that tells me she's on to my scheming ways.

After lunch, we all take a rest on the lounge chairs in our cabana. The girls veg out with the iPad and a Disney movie while Jillian dives back into reading her book. I kick back with my phone in hand, perusing social media and such, when my phone pings with a text message from one of my best friends and teammates.

Justin: What's up? You back in town yet?

Derek: Nope. Sitting in a cabana at the moment. What are you up to?

Justin: Just chilling. Was going to go hit up TopGolf and wanted to see if you wanted to meet me there, but that isn't going to happen.

Derek: Not today, but I'll hit you up when we get back. My parents are on their way to spend the next few days with us here. I've worn Jillian down and she agreed to a date, so that's happening.

Justin: Tell me how is it that you're still pussy whipped when you're not even tapping it?

Derek: Just a matter of time, man. Patience is key and I've got the patience of a fucking saint. That, and I had her coming on my dick the other night. Not exactly how I'd wanted her coming as there was three layers of fabric between us, but at least she let me touch her.

Justin: Damn dude. Well, I hope it pans out for you. You know I've always liked Jillian. She's a cool chick. Has to be to put up with your moody ass.

Derek: You'll find the right woman one of these days and you'll realize that she's worth moving mountains for. And I'll have a blast watching you fall, my man.

Justin: I'm good with the single life. No need to tie myself down.

Derek: I'll remind you of this conversation when the inevitable happens.

Justin: Later fucker.

Derek: Later.

We've waited long enough to safely return to the pool since eating, so I grab both girls and we take off for the water once again. They jump off the side of the pool and ride the slides so many times I lose count. We're all finally exhausted from the time in the water and sun, so we call it an afternoon and head back up to our room. My parents will be here soon, so I jump in the shower to wash off the chlorine and sunscreen from the day, then head down to the lobby to meet them and bring them up. I was able to secure the suite next to ours for them, so it makes it easy and convenient.

"I've got your surprise!" I call out a short while later as I open the suite door, getting their attention. I hold the door open for my parents to walk through and the girls immediately spring up when they see them.

"Nana! Papa!" they both call out as they run to give them hugs.

"What a surprise!" Jill says, standing to hug my parents.

"We were thrilled when Derek called us the other day and asked if we'd like to fly down. He took care of all the arrangements. All we had to do was pack a bag and get ourselves to the airport this morning," Mom tells Jill.

"Well, I'm glad that you could join us. We've been having a great time."

"From the pictures you've posted so far, it looks like an amazing week so far," my mom says.

I touch my mom's arm. "Your suite is the one right next door, so you don't have far to go."

"We still need to check in," my dad says.

"Since I booked everything last-minute, they couldn't send you the magic bands in the mail, but they assured me they'd have them for you guys at check-in."

"That's fine. So, what's the plan for the rest of the day?" Mom asks, mainly to Jill.

"Today was a down day for us. We spent most of it at the pool. We actually just came back up about forty-five minutes ago. We'll probably be ready to head to dinner in about an hour, so if you guys want to go get all checked in and unpacked, we can go once you're done."

"Sounds perfect," Mom tells her.

"I'll head down with you guys to make sure there's no issues with the check-in process," I say, then lead the way.

"Did you get your parents all settled?" Jillian asks after I return to the room.

"I did. The front desk had everything ready and waiting for them. They were going to unpack and freshen up before coming over so we can head for dinner soon."

"Oh, good. I'm starving!"

"Yeah, me too. All that time in the pool really did me in today. I'm just as tired as I've been from walking around in the parks all day," I state.

"That's why I planned for a down day. I knew we'd be exhausted from all the long days."

"Smart idea, for sure. Are we just planning on heading down to the restaurant in the hotel tonight?"

"Either that, or we can order in something if you don't want to go out."

"Let's do that. Then everyone can be comfortable, and no crowds," I reply. "Do we have a menu we can order from?"

"I think so, let me check." Jillian walks over to the desk in the room. She opens a binder and flips through the pages. "Here it is. Pretty much anything we could potentially want," she says, handing it over to me. I send my mom a quick text.

Derek: Jillian and I were just talking about dinner and think we'd all just stay in and order. Do you guys want to look at the menu and let me know what you want so we can order it.

M+D: Sounds good to us. I'll pull it out and take a look. Dad is in the shower, so it will be a few minutes before he can look it over.

Derek: No problem.

M+D: I'll take the Caesar Salad with grilled shrimp, as well as an extra order of grilled shrimp, please. I'll either report back with Dad's or he can just give it to you once we're over there after he's done showering.

Derek: Got it down.

"Mom already gave me her order. Dad's will be along shortly," I tell Jillian. I jot down on a sheet of paper Mom's order, as well as my own and hand it over, so she can put her own down, as well as what she thinks the girls will want.

"Move over," I tell Addison as I attempt to squeeze myself between my girls. "Daddy wants to snuggle."

They allow me to squeeze in, then quickly plaster themselves to my sides as they snuggle up. There's nothing like being pinned down by two little girls. Nothing compares to this, and I wouldn't change it for anything.

SIXTEEN

JILLIAN

"I MIGHT HAVE HAD ULTERIOR MOTIVES WHEN I invited my parents to join us," Derek tells me as we sit out on the balcony, a glass of wine in my hand and a beer in his.

I look over at him, raising my eyebrows in question. "And that would be what?"

A smirk tugs at the corner of his lips. Those damn kissable lips I've had to keep myself from kissing whenever I want.

"That date that you agreed to go on with me. I didn't want to wait until we got back home, so tomorrow night, the girls will hang out with my parents while we go out."

I set my wine glass down on the little table between us, a little flabbergasted he'd bring his parents all the way to Florida just so we can go out on a date. "Are you serious?"

"As a heart attack," he says, pinning me with his eyes.

"I-I just don't know what to say. The fact that you brought your parents here last-minute, were able to secure the suite next to us, everything that goes into being here for multiple days." I suck in a deep breath, allowing myself a few moments to let what he's just said sink in. "All so, what, we can go on a date?"

"Pretty much," he states, matter-of-factly. "I didn't want to give you the chance to back out, or for us to get home and things to get busy, and it not happen. So, I pulled some strings, and *made* things happen. I figured this was a good use of my celebrity status and bank account balance." He laughs lightly.

"I guess so."

"So, Jillian, will you do me the honors of going out with me tomorrow night?"

"Yes, I'll go out with you on a date," I agree, and the butterflies start their dancing in my belly, just as they did all those years ago when I finally gave in to his request for a date in college.

"You look beautiful. Has Derek told you where he's taking you yet?" my former mother-in-law, Elizabeth, asks me after I exit the bathroom, where I was applying some makeup and fixing my hair.

"Nope. He's kept it a secret. Did he tell you?"

"Nope. That boy of mine has been tight-lipped."

"He's up to something, that's for sure."

"All for a good cause," she says, a hopeful hint to her voice and facial expression.

I've always gotten along great with his family. They welcomed me in with open arms the first time we met, after Derek and I had been dating for a few months. They've always been that perfect extended family, supportive when we needed it, yet allowing us to make our own path in life.

"Are you ready to go?" Derek asks. I look over my

shoulder to see him leaning against the doorway, and do my best to give him a cheeky reply, but it falls flat as his appearance jumbles my thoughts. The bastard knows damn well what it does to me when he wears a pair of slacks and button-down with the sleeves rolled up to his elbows. The sinewy muscles of his forearms make my ovaries scream. I'm liable to turn into a pile of drool if I'm not careful.

"Yes," I finally push out, more breathily than I'd hoped to answer him.

"Let's go then." He holds out a hand for me to grab, and I'm not sure if he's offering it to me in support because he knows I'll be on shaky legs after seeing him dressed this way, or if it's because he wants to touch me. Either way is perfectly fine with me, at the moment. He could toss me over his shoulder and take me directly to his bed and I wouldn't complain right now.

"Have fun, you two!" Elizabeth calls out. "We won't wait up for you, and we'll get up with the girls in the morning, so enjoy your night."

"Thanks, Mom," Derek calls over his shoulder as he opens our suite door, escorting me out.

"So, where are you taking me?" I ask as we ride the elevator down to the first floor.

"Dinner, then a stroll through the different countries as we sample wine from each of them."

"That sounds perfect," I tell him as I allow him to link his fingers with mine. We exit the main doors and one of the bellmen greets us by name.

"Mr. and Mrs. Smyth, your ride is right this way." We follow behind him and I gasp when I see the Cinderella-like carriage waiting for us to climb up into.

Once we're settled, the driver gives instructions to the horses pulling us and we take off for the restaurant.

"I never knew you could take a carriage ride here."

"Yep. This route might have been a special request, but they aim to please, so it wasn't all that hard to arrange," he tells me, speaking directly into my ear, as if there might be anyone around who could be listening in on our conversation.

I take in the sights as we make our way to the restaurant, where we are once again given the royal treatment. Derek did good when it came to pulling out all the stops tonight.

"Tell me. What's one thing I can do that will help you with letting me move back home?" Derek asks as we walk around Epcot and through the different countries. His question takes me a little by surprise, so I ponder it for a few minutes while we walk in silence.

"I don't really know how to answer that question. It's not just a simple flippant decision."

"And I understand that. But I think I've proven to the both of us that when I'm determined, I can make changes, and have stuck to those changes."

"I agree with that statement, but it's also been the offseason. What happens when February rolls around and you have to report to pitchers and catchers camp? What happens when you're in the middle of the season and out on the road for a week, and the guys all want to party it up? Those are the moments I dread the most. And I'm not saying that you can't go out and have a good time with your friends and teammates, I'd never say you couldn't spend time with them, but you allowed those times to get out of control in the past, and I just worry that history will repeat itself when you're put back in that situation."

"I understand your position and concerns. And I can't tell you exactly what's going to happen when I'm put in those situations. But I can promise you that I wouldn't do anything to mess up what I've worked so damn hard at all these months. When the judge smacked her gavel against her desk that day, it was like my heart was ripped from my chest. Being told that my family was no longer my family just about killed me, Jillian. And I'll be damned if I don't do everything in my power to get it back and keep it. All three of you, with me always."

He tugs on my hand, pulling me to a stop and angling my body so I'm standing in front of him. His hands cup my cheeks as he looks into my eyes. The serious expression, the fire in his eyes, tells me all I need to know. Every word he's spoken tonight is from his heart. He means it and won't go against his word.

"Just think about it, please," he says, a hint of desperation in his voice. His forehead rests against my own as we stand here in the middle of a country, the world around us fading out to background noise. All I can hear in this instant is our slightly labored breathing as we both keep the eye contact, not wanting to break it and mess with this moment. "Please, just give me another chance. I love you with my entire being. Mind, body, and soul. I'm nothing if not yours. You complete me, Jillian. You and those two precious girls that you gave me."

"Okay," I tell him, no longer able to hold the emotion back.

"Okay?" he questions, right before slamming his lips against my own in a searing and demanding kiss. He deepens the kiss without coming up for more air. He lifts me off my feet, continuing to kiss me deeply. I stop myself from wrapping my legs around his hips, seeing that we are still out in public. That, and if I did that, I don't think my dress would keep things covered, and the last thing we need is to get arrested at freaking Disney World for indecent exposure. His manager and public relations people would have a field day with those kinds of charges.

He finally breaks his lips away from mine and sets me back down on my feet. "I love you," he says, dropping one last chaste kiss against my lips.

"I love you, too," I tell him, a huge smile covering my kiss-swollen lips.

"I won't make you regret it." He slips his fingers back in between my own and we walk through the rest of the countries, drinking wine, talking and laughing as we stroll aimlessly. I don't even really take in the sights, as I'm so drawn into our conversation that is about anything and everything, yet nothing at the same time. Just random things that pop into our heads. It's like talking with no filter. We were always like this when we were young, and this moment takes me back all those years when we'd have plenty of day-dates and would wander with no destination in mind.

"Are you ready to head back?" I ask, a yawn escaping my lips.

"I am if you are," Derek says, tucking me into his side as we head for the exit.

"I am exhausted." I look down at my watch. "Holy crap, it's almost midnight. No wonder I'm so tired."

"We'll be back to the hotel shortly," he says, escorting me to the monorail entrance. "I was going to book the carriage back to the hotel but figured this was faster."

"Good thinking." I lean against his chest as we pick a place to stand while it takes us back to the hotel.

We quietly make it into our suite, where the lights are all dimmed, and the space is quiet. I walk into the kitchen area to grab a bottle of water. I find a note on the counter and pick it up to read it.

The girls did great tonight. They're fast asleep in the extra bedroom in our suite. We hope you kids had a great night out. Now enjoy the empty suite. Call us when you're up and moving tomorrow and we can pick a place to meet if we've already left with the girls. Love M&D.

"Your parents have the girls," I tell Derek over my shoulder. He walks up behind me, slipping a hand around my midsection, bringing it to rest against my stomach.

"I know." He pushes the hair off my neck as he brings his lips to the area. As soon as his lips connect with my skin, a jolt of awareness shoots straight to my center. My clit starts pulsing immediately and I turn my neck just a tad bit to give him a little more access. He sucks at my rapid-beating pulse, sending yet another shiver down my body. "Let me take you to bed," his gravelly voice rasps in my ear.

Between the butterflies before we left tonight, and everything he put into motion for this date night to happen, to his searing kiss a little while ago, and his touch and kisses now, it all has my body on fire and ready to detonate. "Mhmmm." I hum my agreement to his question.

"I need your words, baby," he tells me, tugging my earlobe between his teeth.

"Yes," I finally moan out.

That's all it takes, and he whisks me off to the bedroom. I faintly register the door closing behind us as he kicks at it after we walk through. There is a king-size bed in this room, and he doesn't stop moving until he's standing at the edge of it and has me laid back in the center. His hands slide up my legs, under the hem of my dress, halting at the edge of my panties. They skim over them, causing my center to throb in anticipation and want. I can feel my panties getting damper as the seconds tick by.

"You're so wet for me," he muses as he strokes his fingers

over the outside of my panties, sliding the backs of his fingers up and down my slit.

"Derek," I whine, hoping he'll move this torture along and give us what we both want.

"Tell me what you want."

"You," I manage to tell him as he slips his fingers under the edge of my panties and inside me. I almost come right then in that moment. It's been way too long since I've had him inside me, and these are only his damn fingers. He removes them just as quick and the whimper that falls from my lips tells him how much I disapprove of his actions.

"Patience, baby." He laughs, then tugs my panties down my legs before dropping his trousers and boxers.

I sit up and help him unbutton his dress shirt, then push it off his shoulders. God, his muscles make me stupid some-times, and this moment is one of them. I kiss a line from his chest to the happy trail that leads down his belly.

"That will have to wait," he tells me as he pushes me back on the bed. We've effectively rid each other of all our clothes in the last minute or so. I was so distracted by him I don't even recall how he got my dress off of me, but it's gone, so it happened. "What should I do to you first?" His hand comes back to my center. He rolls his fingertips around my clit, just not applying pressure directly on it, not giving in to what I want.

"I don't care, just hurry the fuck up," I tell him.

"Yes, ma'am," he replies, and lowers himself between my thighs. One flick of his tongue against my center and I'm already seeing stars. He follows my body's cues and works me over. Every lick, kiss, flick, is done in a way to prolong my pleasure. I unravel against his tongue multiple times before he slides up my body and slides his gloriously hard cock inside of me. As he settles his entire length in me, his lips find mine in a searing kiss, and he stills for a moment.

"Move," I pant against his lips once I've had time to adjust. He starts slow, sliding out until just the crown of his cock is left inside and then thrusts in, hard and fast. His hips pump, pinning mine into the mattress at a punishing pace. One my body is ready to take. One it has craved for months. The electric connection between the two of us returns, as if we'd never been apart. The way we know each other's bodies, only the way two longtime lovers can. As much as make-up sex can be cathartic for couples, this is that on steroids. The time we've spent apart built up that anticipation. The sexual tension that has been bouncing around between is also playing into tonight.

"I need you there," Derek grits out as he changes his angle slightly and the tempo of his thrusts. "I'm so close, and need you coming with me." He kisses me hard, slipping his hand between us. The moment the pad of his thumb finds my clit, I come apart and fall over the cliff. Earth-shattering, stars fill my vision. I forget how to breathe with the amount of pleasure rolling through my body at this moment. I vaguely realize Derek is falling over his own cliff, and his hips snap one last time before he spills inside of me. I can feel each jet of his cum as it leaves his body. A fleeting second of panic rolls through my brain as I think about my birth control, but I remember I took it this morning at my normal time, as always.

We stay in this position, Derek's head resting on the bed just above my shoulder as we both recover. "That was..." He trails off, his lips against my skin.

"Magical," I offer up.

"Yes, and so much more," he finally says. He starts to slip out of me, then stands and grabs a tissue from the nightstand to try and keep from creating a wet spot on the bed. I sit up, staying put for a moment so I don't blackout from standing so quickly. Once I know I'll be fine, I make my way into the bathroom to clean up, and Derek steps inside with me. "Take a shower with me?"

"Sure," I agree to his request. No sense in regretting what we just did now.

SEVENTEEN

DEREK

I flick the hot water on as Jillian goes to the bathroom. It only takes it a moment for the water to warm up, so I slip under it while I wait for her to join me. I tip my head forward, closing my eyes as the hot water beats on my neck and shoulders. It felt so fucking good to slip into her tonight. Something I've longed to do for months now, and my patience and hard work paid off. I've hopefully proven to her I've changed my ways, and I'm here to be the man she needs. The positive role model our girls need in their lives, so when the time comes for them to start dating, they hope-fully find men who will support them, challenge them, but most of all, love and respect them like they deserve to be.

My thoughts are interrupted as Jillian's hands connect with my abs, then wrap around my back as she joins me under the water. I immediately pull her against me, our bodies flush. I tip her chin up and capture her lips with mine, threading my fingers into her wet hair as I angle her head so I can easily deepen the kiss. I swallow the moans I can feel vibrating from her throat, as she does the same with mine.

I back her up against the tiled wall, hooking one of her legs around my hip. I'm already hard once again, and ready to go, but I take my time kissing her, enjoying every second of the intimacy that is so freely flowing between the two of us. Intimacy always came easy to us; we each learned the other's likes and dislikes fairly quick in the early months of our relationship. Way back before kids. Back when we couldn't keep our hands off of each other. When we'd fuck any moment we had the chance.

I thrust against her pussy now that the wall is supporting her back. This position gives me the perfect angle to tease her until she can't take it anymore.

"Derek!" she shrieks as our lips break apart.

My lips find the column of her neck, and I suck hard as my cock slides right across her clit. I can feel her pulse thrumming hard against the head as I do, and know she's close to coming again.

"That's it, baby," I whisper into her ear. "Come for me." I thrust my cock along her clit a couple more times until I feel her let go and fall over the cliff. "That's it, beautiful."

I continue to murmur into her hair as she collapses against my chest. Once I feel her relax, I lift her chin so she's looking at me again. "I love you, and I'm going to show you that all night long."

I slam my lips against hers as I cup her ass with both of my hands, lifting her up until she's got both of her legs wrapped around my torso. I grab my aching cock in hand, give it a few tugs before lining it up with her pussy and thrusting home once again. My hips piston into her, my balls already tightening after the first few thrusts. I can't stop my orgasm from barreling down my spine.

"Fuck, Jillian!" I yell as I empty myself inside her once again.

It takes me a couple of minutes to regain myself; for my breathing to return to normal and my vision to focus on my surroundings. I haven't come that hard in years. "Are you okay?" I ask as I slip from Jill's body. I hold on to her until I'm confident she has the strength to stand on her own.

"Perfect," she assures me as she kisses my chest. The moment her lips connect with my skin, I realize just how much I've missed her like this. Missed her lips against my skin, missed her casual touches, and being able to touch her whenever I want, just because.

I love how her body reacts as my hands slip over her skin while I lather the body wash. No words are needed as we slip into a comfortable silence. We each feed off the cues our bodies give each other.

Once we're both cleaned, I turn the water off and grab one of the big, fluffy towels and wrap it around Jillian, then pull her back to me to place a chaste kiss against her lips. "I'll meet you in bed."

"We need one of those." She points to the heated towel rack.

"Done." I didn't miss how she said *we*, nor am I going to point it out right now. "I'll order one from Amazon tomorrow."

She smiles at me over her shoulder before walking out of the bathroom. I grab my own towel and quickly dry off before following her into the bedroom. I watch from a distance as she sits on the edge of the bed and rubs on her favorite lotion, and it hits me once again how much I missed these simple moments between the two of us. How intimate things like this can be, and how much of an ass I was to take it all for granted, then throw it all away so easily for something as stupid as partying it up with my single teammates and friends. Allowing the fame to become more important than staying in with my wife and kids, spending the quiet downtime with Jillian, making memories that would last well past my playing days.

Once she shuts the lotion bottle and sets it aside, I close the distance between where I stood and the bed. I pull the covers back, drop the towel from around my waist, and slide between the sheets. I pull the blankets back on her side and pat the bed next to my side. "Come here."

I watch her every movement, and the way her eyes flick to mine as she bites her bottom lip. I take in her calculated, slow—way too fucking slow, if you ask me—movements as she slowly lifts her hand to the top of the towel tucked in between her breasts. My mouth waters as I wait for it to drop to the floor. The anticipation is killing me. Even though I've seen her naked thousands of times over the years and was *just* inside her minutes ago—twice tonight already—the anticipation is still high. My breath catches as her fingers finally, *finally*, pull the top of the towel free and she lets go of it. It quickly drops to the floor with a *whoosh*. She stands only a few feet from me, naked and beautiful.

"So fucking beautiful," I growl as I hold my hand up for her to grab.

"You know, you already got me into bed, you don't have to try and charm me anymore," she says as she takes my hand and slides into bed next to me.

"I'm not trying to charm you, sweetheart. I'm just telling you the truth. You are fucking beautiful. The most beautiful woman I've ever seen, the only one I *want* to see." I tug her closer to me. "The only one who can make me hard in a second flat," I tell her as I grab her hand and wrap it around my hard cock.

"Just by biting this bottom lip." I slide the pad of my thumb along her lip, pulling it from beneath her teeth. "I've never been so jealous of someone biting a lip before in my life."

"You're incorrigible," she says, laughing and smacking her free hand against my chest. Her other hand—the one still wrapped around my cock—squeezes me slightly before she starts to lazily stroke me from root to tip, driving me fucking crazy. I bite my tongue to keep from telling her to speed up her movement, as I want her in charge, to see what she wants right now.

I roll onto my back when Jillian pushes against my chest, and rest my hands behind my head. I'm trying really hard to not take control, and keeping my hands pinned will at least slow me down from trying.

I watch her every move, from the way her hand looks wrapped around my aching cock, to how her body slides down the length of my body. Her lips map the ridges of my abs and they quake under her touch. The way she so expertly moves across each ridge and valley of my muscles, knowing exactly where to place her lips to drive me fucking crazy.

"Jill, baby." I groan just as her lips wrap around the crown of my cock. "Fuuuuuck," falls from my lips as she takes me deep into her mouth. The tip of my cock hits the back of her throat and she hums around me. The vibrations send chills up my spine and have my balls tightening. I'm like a fucking, horny-ass, fifteen-year-old getting his first blow job tonight with the way I'm ready to shoot off, and I've come twice already in the last hour alone. This woman is going to be the death of me.

She ignores my pleas as she tortures me with her heaven-sent mouth. I grind my back teeth together, start thinking about anything to keep myself from losing control and coming down her throat too quickly. When the only action I've seen in months is my hand, my body is going crazy after tonight's events.

"Jillian..." I growl one last time, giving in and wrapping my hands around her arms to tug her up. "I can't hold off much longer," I tell her as she returns to stroking my cock with her hand. The sexy-ass grin she shoots me tells me she knows exactly how close I am to blowing my load, and it also tells me that's exactly what she's after.

"Then come, Derek," she finally says, having increased the speed and tightness of her strokes.

"Roll over, I'm going to come all over your tits."

"But we just showered."

"We can shower again later," I grit out. "Or I can slide back into that tight pussy of yours and come inside you once again."

She must like that suggestion because before I can even finish my sentence, she's straddling my hips and lowering herself onto my cock. I grab hold of her hips and thrust up as she falls down, until I'm balls deep and can't get any further inside her. Her walls flutter around me at the roughness. I don't give her much time as I withdraw and thrust back up over and over again, our pace frantic as I chase another orgasm for both of us. The more her body shudders around my cock like this, the more my balls pull up and that tingle starts once more. With one final thrust, I give in and let it go. I slam her back down on my cock and empty every last drop I can muster up into her. Her body does delicious things as it comes apart on top of me, and I can feel everything.

EIGHTEEN

JILLIAN

I COLLAPSE FORWARD, MY HEAD RESTING RIGHT OVER Derek's heart. My body is fluid and relaxed from all the hormones flooding my bloodstream. Neither of us can get enough of the other. That small little clasp of control finally gave way tonight and it's like we were taken back to our college years. Back to before we had kids and adult problems. Back to when our only concerns were sex, school, and baseball. Oh, to have such small problems once again.

My breathing finally slows, yet I make no attempt to move. I feel so perfect right here in Derek's arms, his body practically engulfing mine. He holds every last ounce of my weight so effortlessly, and most of all, I feel so loved and protected in this moment.

I let the steady thump of his heartbeat lull me into a sleepy daze. I don't completely fall under, but I'm very close to that edge with us like this.

"Baby, you still awake?" His whisper breaks the silence as his hand coasts up and down my back.

"Mhmmm."

"We need to get cleaned back up before we can fall

asleep," he tells me, and I can feel him start to slip out of me. He's right, but that doesn't make me want to move any more than I did a few seconds ago.

"Okay." I finally give in as he attempts to move closer to the edge of the bed. I sit up and look down at him, and can see complete satisfaction in his eyes. The darkness that had settled in over the past couple of months is gone. It's like his entire demeanor has changed after tonight. I knew us being apart was hard on him, but I don't think I realized just how difficult it had been until seeing him now. It's almost like an entire weight has been lifted off his shoulders. I always had faith he could turn things around and realize he wasn't living the life he'd always wanted to. Wasn't living up to his normal standards he'd once set to be as a loving and loyal family man.

He stands and scoops me into his arms, then heads for the bathroom once again.

I giggle. "Put me down, I can walk."

"This was faster," he insists as we reach the bathroom door. I flip the light on as he steps through, then sets me on the tile floor.

"Crap, the floor is cold," I whine.

"Then, the faster you are in here, the faster you can get back into bed and I'll warm you up." He winks at me as he grabs a washcloth to clean himself off. I quickly take care of my own things in the bathroom before heading back to bed. My body is well sated and is going to be sore tomorrow in ways I haven't been in years. But it was all worth it. I can only hope I've gotten back the man I fell for all those years ago. The man who I once pledged to spend the rest of my life with, for better or worse. While death didn't pull us apart, I hope in the future, that's the only thing that will.

I WAKE UP AND ATTEMPT TO ROLL OVER TO SEE WHAT time it is, but can't due to the large body wrapped around me and holding me tight. "Derek." My voice is groggy as I try to wiggle free from his hold. "Derek, I need to get up," I state, a little more sternly.

"Not yet," he says in his sleep, tightening his hold on me.

I elbow him in the ribs. "Yes, yet."

"Ouch," he grunts.

"Sorry, but I've got to pee, and *now*." He finally loosens his grip and I slip from the bed. I glimpse at the clock as I dash for the bathroom and can't believe it's already almost ten in the morning.

"Are you coming back to bed?" he asks when I come out of the bathroom.

"I don't think so. It's already ten. I can't believe we haven't heard from your parents or the girls yet."

"Mom said not to worry about them, that they'd handle everything this morning and to just call them when we were ready to meet up. So, get your ass back in bed. I wasn't done holding you."

"Is that so?" I saunter back over to the edge of the bed.

"Sure is." He tugs me down onto the mattress and back under the covers, where he engulfs me once again with his large, warm body.

I snuggle up, tucked against his side. His arm comes around my back with his hand settling on my hip, his fingers drawing lazy circles on my skin.

"Are you hungry?" I ask, since I'm starving.

"Yes," he tells me as his stomach starts to make growling noises.

"I guess so." I laugh. "How about I grab the room service menu and we put in an order. We can get ready while we wait for the food, then go find our family to meet up with for the rest of the day?"

"If you insist. I'd be happy with some food and spending the rest of the day in bed," he says, nuzzling my neck. His lips find my one downfall spot just under my ear.

"As lovely as that sounds, we've got kids to tend to. We can't just leave them to your parents all day."

"Actually, we can." His hand cups my breast and he rolls my nipple between the pads of his fingers, and it sends tingles right to my core. "Mom said to take all the time we needed. They're perfectly happy to spoil the girls all day. Have some grandparent-granddaughter bonding time."

"You make it sound so appealing," I say as I angle my body, so he has better access.

"I can guarantee you that it will be well worth it for you if you stay here with me today," he says, a cocky-as-shit grin on his lips as he looks me dead in the eye before he flips us so I'm on my back under him. His lips wrap around my nipple and he nips and licks at it, driving me fucking wild.

"Derek," I pant as his tongue flicks at my sensitive peak.

"Yes, baby?"

"Food. We need food." I somehow remember how to speak.

"I've got all the food I need right in front of me."

"Fucking funny," I deadpan. "I need sustenance."

"Fine," he says, sitting up, and I immediately miss his tongue and lips on my nipples. A small whimper falls from my lips and he doesn't miss it.

"Plenty more for you later. But first, food." He slides off the bed and stalks over to the desk to look for the room service menu.

"I think the menus are out in the kitchen area," I tell him as he moves things around, not finding what he wants.

"Of course," he says under his breath, yet still loud enough I can hear him. I watch as he looks around on the floor until he locates his boxers. He slips them up his legs and then heads out of the room. When he opens the door, the suite appears to be silent, so I take that as a good sign his parents are out somewhere with the girls or still have them in their suite next door.

He comes back a minute or so later with a binder from the kitchen. He sits down on the bed next to me and flips it open to the breakfast menu. I read the options from over his shoulder. Once we've both made our selections, I call the order in for us.

"How about a shower while we wait?" he asks.

"I think *separate* showers while we wait sounds perfect," I tell him, deflating him just a smidge.

"I don't like that option," he protests.

"I'm sure you don't, but we both know that if we get into that shower together, it's going to turn into a dirty shower and we might miss the food being delivered. I don't know about you, but after the workout you put me through last night, I've worked up an appetite and I'm bordering on being hangry. So, back that horny man up. You're not touching me with that cock until I've been given some sustenance."

"You're cute when you're determined." He pulls me in for a chaste kiss. "But I know better than to come between you and your food. So, food, then a shower, and maybe another round of shower sex before we have to face the day for a few hours."

I drop a chaste kiss against his lips. "Sounds like a plan I can get behind."

NINETEEN

DEREK

We've been home from vacation for a little over a week and life has been just about as perfect as I could have asked for. Jillian has stayed open to the idea of us happening again. She's let me stay at the house, back in our bed. The multiple orgasms I've been so expertly providing each night haven't hurt my cause. But, the ultimate test will come in a few more weeks, when I have to return to work. Pitchers and catchers have to report first before the rest of the team, and training is held down in Arizona. So that means time away from my girls. Time around the guys. Distance from my girls. Hopefully that time and distance won't stop the progress we've made.

I roll over in bed, reaching for Jillian's warm body. I find her curled up on the edge of her side, and I pull her back to the center of the bed and into my embrace. I nuzzle my nose into her hair, taking in a deep breath. Her scent fills my lungs and my body relaxes like I've just taken a hit of some drug. She's the only drug I need, the only one I've ever taken or needed.

"What time is it?" she mumbles.

"About five a.m. Go back to sleep," I tell her as I slip my hand around her hip and onto her belly. My fingertips slide under the tank top she's got on, resting once they're fully under it and on her skin.

"Why are you awake then?" she asks, shifting slightly in my embrace.

"You were too far away from me."

"Mhmmm." She hums as she falls back to sleep.

I lay here with her back plastered to my front, like two spoons perfectly seated together. Her body fits so perfectly against my own and I wish I could keep us in this moment forever. I tuck it away so I can think back on it when my nights will be lonely once I'm back at work and away from her.

WITH ME DUE TO TRAINING CAMP IN JUST ANOTHER couple of weeks, it's time I quit slacking off this offseason and get back into game shape, so I head for the gym. When I arrive, a few other of the guys had the same thoughts as I did, and I find a handful of my teammates already here working out. After dropping my bag in my locker bay, I make my way out to the weight room. I find my best friend, JJ, already here and getting started.

"Hey, man," I greet him, pounding the fist he holds out to me after he finishes his rep of squats.

"How's it hanging?"

"Eh, it's hanging. I'm ready to get back in the swing of things."

"Me too, bro. How're Jillian and the girls?" he asks between sets.

"Good," I tell him with a smile on my lips. "Things are

really good. Disney was just what we needed, even if it did cost me a fortune."

"Please, like your bank account even felt the hit," he replies, smirking at me. It's no secret I'm one of the highest paid pitchers in the league.

"Dude, I could have bought a car for the amount that we dropped. But I'd do it ten times over if it got me to where we are again."

"Then it sounds like money well spent."

"What are we focusing on today?" I ask, changing the subject to what we both came here to do.

"Figured a full body workout was the place to start. I know I've gone slack this offseason a bit more than I should have."

"I know what you mean." I nod in agreement as we both start hitting the weights. We've been doing this long enough we know what we need to work on.

Two and a half hours later, I'm dripping in sweat and ready to collapse on the floor. My body is screaming at me for the workout I've subjected it to after so long off, but with pain comes improvement and strength. Strength is something I need to make it through the long season and hopefully late into the postseason. To be playing baseball come September and October is always the dream of every professional baseball player, and I know my years of that happening are definitely numbered.

"Want to go grab some lunch?" JJ asks once we're both showered off and dressed.

"Sure. Mexican?" I ask. My old agent, Madison, turned me on to this little Mexican joint her husband and his old teammates like to go to all the time.

"Sounds good. I could go for a good margarita right about now," JJ comments. "I'll meet you there."

I pull my cell phone from my pocket and send off a quick text to Jillian to let her know what my plans are.

Derek: JJ and I are going out for lunch. Need me to pick up anything afterwards before I come home?

Jillian: We're good here. How was your workout this morning?

Derek: Kicked my ass but felt good to get back to the gym. No more slacking off for me if I'm going to be ready for training camp next month.

Jillian: I'm sure you'll be ready. It's not like you let your body go.

Derek: You're good for my ego, babe. :winky face:

Jillian: Is that all I'm good for?

Derek: Fuck no. You're good for so much more.... I'll prove it to you tonight.

Jillian: I'll hold you to that.

My cock hardens in my pants at the thought of her holding me to do *anything*, but damn, do I love it. I love that we're back to this easy banter, the ease of knowing each other so well.

I slip my phone back in my pocket as I reach my truck. I toss my bag in the back seat and climb in, then take off for the restaurant. It doesn't take me long to get there and find a parking spot. I pull in next to JJ's swanky sports car. I swear the guy changes cars as often as some people change their underwear.

"When did you get this ride?" I ask, checking out the sleek car.

"Last week," he says, taking in the beauty of the car that is in front of us. I feel my phone buzz in my pocket, so I pull it out while we walk into the restaurant.

I see Riley's picture flashing on the screen and slide the button across to answer her call.

"Hey, Ry," I greet her by her nickname.

"Hello to you, my big brother."

"What do I owe the pleasure of your call?" I ask as JJ and I walk through the doors.

"Can't I just call my brother every once in a while?" she asks, but I can tell something is behind her call.

"You know you can call me anytime."

"I know. How are the girls? Did they have fun at Disney? Mom said it was a blast," she asks, hardly stopping for air between questions.

"They're good and they loved it. Do you think you can take some time off anytime soon and come out and see them? I can get you a ticket, and you know you can stay at the house."

"Well, actually, I had a favor to ask," she says, finally getting to the reason for her call.

"What's that?" I ask as we're led to a table.

"My job kind of fell through this week. I don't really like it here, so I was thinking maybe I could move out there around you guys, find a job there. That would allow me to see all of you more often, and I wouldn't be out here in Ohio all by myself."

"Of course. You can stay at the house, or better yet, I've

still got my condo and we can just move you into that. I had to sign a year lease, so that gives you another six, seven months to decide if you like that area."

"Really?!"

"Absolutely. You know we'd do anything we can to help you. Jillian and the girls will be excited to see more of you, I'm sure."

"You're the best, Derek."

"When do you want to come? And do you need me to get you a ticket?"

"Can I arrive this weekend?" she asks apprehensively.

"Of course."

"Whew. I've got my apartment about three-fourths the way packed, and most of my furniture sold off or donated. I wanted to pull out and drive down in the next few days."

"Do you need me to fly up and help you?"

"No, I should be okay to drive it by myself. It isn't that far, only about five hours or so."

"Okay. Well, if that changes, let me know. I'll let Jillian know what the plan is, and to expect you this weekend."

"Thanks, Derek."

"Anytime, Ry. Love you."

"Love you, too, see you soon."

At that, we hang up, and I flip open the menu in front of me.

"Your sister, I take it?" JJ says from across the table.

"Yep. Something happened with her new job, and she's not enjoying Ohio, so she's going to move down here to be around family."

"I don't blame her. I wouldn't want to be in Ohio, either." He grimaces.

I laugh at his antics. "It can't be that bad."

"I've not spent much time there, but what I have, it

didn't appeal to me much," he says as our server approaches the table. She takes our drink and food order, then disappears. I look over and see Madison and her husband Richard sitting at a table across the room from us. She's grown a bit since I last saw her, seeing as she's expecting twins here sometime soon.

"I'll be right back," I tell JJ as I stand up and walk over to their table.

"Well, if it isn't the party boy of baseball himself," Madison greets me as I approach.

"Not anymore. I'm putting those days behind me. I've got more important things to focus on," I tell her as I shake Richard's hand. She scoots over to make room for me and I slide in next to her. "How are things going for you?"

"Ugh. I'm as huge as a house, can't breathe half the time, and go from starving to I don't have any more room in the matter of a couple bites of food. Other than that, I'm great."

"When are the babies due?"

"March, but hopefully late February. I don't think I can last much longer than that," she says. "How are Jillian and the girls?"

"Jillian and the girls are doing great. We went to Florida for vacation and it was just what we needed," I tell her honestly. If there's anyone who knows about my life that isn't family, it is Madison. She's been with me for a long-ass time and was one of the best agents in the business. "You sure you're not willing to work part-time? I promise to not be a pain in your ass. I'm a changed man these days."

"I'm sure you are, but no. I'm going to enjoy not dealing with athletes for the next few years."

"Hey!" Richard pipes up from the other side of the table.

"Hush you, I'll always deal with you," she tells her husband with a smile.

"I'll let you guys enjoy your lunch," I say, standing from the table. "Good luck with the babies and all."

"Don't be a stranger, and give my love to Jillian and the girls," Madison tells me. "And, Derek?" I turn my attention back to her. "I'm proud of you. I knew you had it in you to turn things around. Those girls are worth it, I'm sure of it."

"I agree. I'm just the dumbass that had to almost lose everything before he realized just how good he had things."

"Don't beat yourself up too much. We're all human and make mistakes. It's how we learn and change from those mistakes that shows our true colors."

I let her words sink in, waving as I head back to my table. JJ has almost polished off the basket of chips and salsa that was dropped off at our table shortly before I stepped away.

"Save any for me?" I jokingly ask as I sit down.

"Nope," he says, popping the P. Our server arrives just then with a second basket of chips and salsa.

"Your food should be up shortly," she says.

"Thanks," I tell her as she walks away.

We shoot the shit while we eat. JJ tells me about a few of his most recent one-night stands. The man has more notches in his bedpost than Hugh Hefner's playboy mansion.

"You ever going to settle down and get yourself a girl that lasts more than one night?" I ask him after we've paid the bill and head out to the parking lot.

"Where's the fun in that?"

"I could tell you, but you probably wouldn't believe me. Don't you get tired of having to learn what the women you sleep with want or how they respond to what you're doing?"

"Fuck no. They practically beg to take a ride on my cock. You've seen it firsthand. Why would I want to give that up?"

"Because sometimes it's more than just about the pussy."

"And you'd know that, how? If I'm not mistaken, you've been with the same pussy for what, eight years? Did you even sample any before Jillian?"

"That's beside the point. I don't need any other pussy in my life. I'm quite fond of the one I've got," I say, smirking at him.

"Keep telling yourself that, man, and I'll keep sampling it all."

"You're such an asshole."

"You wouldn't have me any other way," he retorts as he opens his car door. "Give my love to Jillian and the girls. I'll see you tomorrow."

"See ya then," I tell him, then climb into my truck and head home.

TWENTY

JILLIAN

Since returning from Florida, things have been so chill and almost too perfect. I keep waiting for the shoe to drop, so to say. I hate that I'm constantly worrying about something happening to change the way things are going for us. Having Derek back in my bed every night and helping around here with mundane things, as well as with the girls so much, has me realizing just how much we were on two completely separate pages for a while.

The last couple of weeks, we've fallen into a new routine. Once the girls are in bed, we sit and relax. We talk so much more than we used to, and not always about serious things, but the time together has made me fall back—or more—in love with Derek than I was before. I've never felt the kind of love for anyone that I do for him. He's my other half. The peanut butter to my jelly, the mac to my cheese. My lobster and the only man I ever want to call my own.

"Honey, I'm home," Derek calls out from the garage door.

"I'm in the kitchen," I reply.

"Hey, beautiful." He comes up behind me, wrapping his

arms around my torso, and pulls me close. His head dips to my neck and his lips find the skin there. "I missed you," he whispers against my skin, and I shiver at the contact.

"How was lunch?" I ask as I finish rinsing off the pan I used to grill the girls their lunch.

"Good, I ran into Madison and Richard. She said to tell you hi."

"How'd she look?"

"Good. Big, but good. Said she's ready for the babies to come."

"I bet." I turn in his arms, then push up on my toes and press my lips against his, catching him by surprise for a second. He quickly melts into my kiss and takes control, and his hands slide up my body quickly until he's cupping my cheeks.

"Love you," he says against my lips once we break the kiss.

"Love you," I reply before lowering back down to my normal height.

"Where are the girls?"

"Napping. Both were in need of one today, so much so that neither of them fought me on it."

"They must have been tired then," he muses. "Oh, before I forget. Ry called me a little while ago. I guess something happened with her job. Since it didn't pan out, she's wanting to move and asked if she could come here. I, of course, told her yes, so she's driving down this weekend. I told her she could stay here, or I was thinking that I could move all my stuff back in and we could just put her up in my condo."

"That sucks about her job, but she's always welcome here. The girls will be ecstatic to see her."

"That's what I told her. So...what do you think about

the apartment?" he asks, obviously nervous about my response to his question. Since we returned from Florida, he hasn't spent one night at the apartment, so it makes sense he just officially move back home. I don't want him anywhere else, and he's definitely proven himself to me.

"I think that sounds like the perfect plan. She'd get tired of staying here after a few days anyways with the craziness of the girls. They'd quickly drive her nuts," I tell him. "Or be the best birth control a girl could ask for."

He growls. "My baby sister doesn't need birth control. She's not dating until she's thirty, just like our girls."

"Oh, please." I roll my eyes as I smack his chest. "Your sister is twenty-two years old. She can date, have S-E-X, even drink if she wants to, and there's nothing you can do to stop her," I say as he shudders. "Please don't tell me you're going to become an over-the-top brother who scares off any guys that try and date her."

"If they can't answer my questions and pass my test, then they aren't dating her."

"Okay then, Mr. Alpha male, overprotective brother. I'll just have to be her kickass sister-in-law who helps her pick out the perfect man to date and drive you nuts with." I cackle at the thought of making him crazy. "Ooh, maybe I can set her up with one of your teammates!"

"Don't you fucking dare."

"Hmmmm... JJ would be a good place to start. That man needs a woman in his life to bring him a little stability and to settle down."

"JJ isn't fucking touching my sister with a goddamn twenty-foot pole, much less anything else," he grits out.

"Oh, come on, Derek," I egg him on. "They'd look so cute together."

"Jillian." He says my name in a demanding tone. "Don't even go there. You know how he is."

"I'm sure he can be tamed."

"Not with my sister," he says, then turns and stalks out of the room.

Well, crap, I didn't mean to piss him off.

"I'M SORRY ABOUT EARLIER TODAY," I TELL DEREK AS I slip between the sheets. "I didn't mean to make you upset about Ry and JJ. I was just trying to tease you."

"I know, and I'm sorry I got so defensive about the whole situation," he says, pulling me into his arms. Tonight, was the first night since we've been back that we didn't sit and talk after the girls went to bed. Derek disappeared after dinner into the home gym we have, only to appear just a little bit ago when I was getting ready for bed. "I'm sorry I didn't help with bedtime tonight. I just needed to clear my mind."

"It's okay. You don't always have to help. I can handle things on my own, ya know. Not that I don't appreciate the help."

"I know you can, but I'm trying to help out as much as I can before I'm gone all the time."

"Yeah." I sigh as I melt into his embrace a little more. "Only a few more weeks until it's back to the grind. Are you excited for the new season?" I ask, pressing a kiss to his chest.

"Yes. I don't think the excitement and anticipation will ever stop and if it does, then it will definitely be time to retire."

"I've never not known you to be like a kid in a candy

store when it was the start of a new season, and I'm glad that you haven't lost that passion for it."

"I sure hope I don't," he says, then falls quiet. "I was thinking about something while working out."

"What's that?"

"With Riley coming here, I'm sure it will take her a few weeks to get settled and find a new job. What if we asked her to watch the girls for a week or so, and you came out to Arizona with me for a little bit of training camp. You can go on hikes during the day, spend some time relaxing at the spa. Just enjoy a little break from being on all the time."

"Oh god, that sounds amazing and something we can talk to her about."

"I think she'd be up for it."

"Or, maybe we could bring her and the girls with, and we can just rent a house and stay for a little longer. It wouldn't be as relaxing, but then it wouldn't be so much on her at one time."

"That'd be an option, as well," he says, dropping a kiss to the top of my head.

TWENTY-ONE

DEREK

THE PAST FEW DAYS HAVE BEEN FILLED WITH MORNING workouts at the team facility with JJ, followed by afternoons with my girls, and then the nights with Jillian naked in bed. We've been a little wild and crazy, not able to get enough of each other. If I don't knock her up again, I'll be a little shocked. The thought of her having another baby, how curvy and luscious she gets when pregnant, turns me right the fuck on. I love how large her tits get, how they overfill my large hands. How, once she hits the second trimester, she's usually so horny she *attacks* me whenever we have a few quiet moments together.

"What's that smirk for?" Her sweet voice breaks me from my daydream as she leans against the bathroom doorway.

"Nothing." I take her in as she stands there with a robe that's open in the middle, showing off her exposed skin. She's only put on a pair of panties. They might block my direct view of her perfect pussy, but I damn well know what it looks like, feels like, fucking tastes like. Dammit, I'm hard once again, and there's no hiding it as my erection tents the sheet that's draped over my legs.

"Mhmmm," she hums, then points at the tent of the sheets and my obvious erection. "Doesn't look like nothing."

"Just thinking about knocking you up again." I smirk at her and wait for her reaction.

"Is that so?" she asks, no shock evident in her voice.

"Mhmmm." I hum right back at her. "You know I can't keep my hands off of you when you're knocked up."

She laughs. "Isn't that the truth."

"So, get your ass over here and let's practice at getting you pregnant."

"How are you ready to go *again*? Wasn't the last *two* times enough *practice*," she says, using air quotes, "for the morning?"

"We can *never* have enough practice." I stand from the bed in all my nakedness. My erection juts out, long and proud, as I close the distance between the two of us. It takes me a few strides since our master bedroom is so fucking big. I back her up against the wall, pinning her there with my hips, then gather both of her hands in one of mine and lift them above her head, holding them against the wall. My other hand trails down her exposed neck, across her collarbone, then dips down between her breasts. I push the robe out of my way, exposing her already hard nipples. I circle them with my fingertips, pinching lightly as I roll them between the pads of my fingers, then dip my head and flick them each with the tip of my tongue. Her breathing quickens as she starts to pant at my teasing.

I take some pity and suck a nipple into my mouth, lavishing it hard. With each flick of my tongue, I notice her legs rub together as she attempts to find some friction. I drop her wrists and lower that hand to her panties. I grip the fabric and pull hard, tearing it from her body.

"Derek!" She gasps at my assertiveness.

"I'll buy you new ones," I state into her skin. "These ones were in my way."

"Such a caveman," she replies on a moan as my fingers find her swollen clit. I flick it with my fingers as my tongue does the same to her nipples. I sink two fingers into her, her muscles fluttering around them as I do. I bring her right to the edge of her orgasm, then pull back, making her crazy as I do so. "Don't be an asshole," she chides as I look at her, the need to come written all over her face.

"Never, sweetheart." I lick her off my fingers, then stand to my full height, pull her leg over my hip, and align my cock with her wet and ready center. I push inside, not stopping until I'm balls deep.

"Fuck!" She screams as I thrust fast, filling her over and over again. I slow only long enough to slip my hands under her ass and lift her up, wrapping her legs around my torso. I keep her pinned against the wall as I unleash inside her. My lips find hers, and I lose myself in her. Between the hold her mouth has on mine and the way my cock feels inside her at this angle, it doesn't take long for me to reach climax. My orgasm sets off hers and we come together against the bathroom wall. Her head falls forward and rests on my shoulder.

"That was..." she says, trailing off.

"Fucking perfect," I finish her sentence.

"Yeah," she agrees a moment later, once she's caught her breath. "We can practice like that anytime you want."

"You liked that, did you?" I chuckle against her skin. I can feel my cock slipping from her, so I slide the rest of the way out and lower her back down to the floor.

"Just a little bit," she says, a coy smile on her lips.

"WHO WANTS TO ANSWER THE DOOR WITH DADDY?" I ask the girls, knowing Riley is at the door. We didn't tell the girls she was coming, wanting to surprise them with her arrival.

"Me!" Addison says, jumping up from the floor where we'd been playing together. I head for the door with both girls in tow. I swing it open and find my baby sister standing there, a huge smile plastered on her face.

"RyRy!" Penelope calls out as soon as she sees my sister. Riley drops to her haunches and opens her arms wide for both of my girls to run into. They just about tackle her, causing her to almost lose her balance as she wraps her arms around both of them at the same time.

"Auntie Ry is here!" she tells both girls as she attempts to stand with both of them still clinging to her neck.

"Why don't you both let Auntie Ry come inside," I say, laughing at my girls' antics.

She adjusts both girls in her arms and walks inside. Neither one of them wanted anything to do with her putting them down, so she forged on.

"How was the drive?" I ask once we've made it into the living room and the girls have allowed her to put them down.

"Uneventful. I got on the road just after breakfast and here I am."

"Do you need some lunch?" Jillian asks, joining us in the living room.

"Maybe in a little bit. I just want to relax for a couple of minutes with these two," she says, getting down on the floor with the girls.

"Did you want to stay here tonight or go get settled in at the apartment?" Jillian asks her.

"Either is fine with me. I don't want to intrude too much on you guys."

"Never. You're always welcome here," Jill replies, just as I knew she would.

"Thanks. And if you ever need a sitter, I'm more than willing to help out. I can't thank you guys enough for letting me come here."

"We're happy to have you."

"Any ideas on what kind of job you want to look for?" I ask, changing the subject.

"It would be nice to get a job in my degree field of Marketing, but those jobs can be hard to come by, as I've found out. So, for now, anything that will pay the bills that is a reputable job."

"What happened with the job you had lined up?" Jill asks.

"My boss was pretty shady and when I declined to become his mistress, he fired me," she says, shrugging her shoulders like it wasn't a big deal.

"He did *what*!?" I yell, the anger radiating off of me.

"He fired me when I told him I wouldn't give him a BJ under his desk between meetings," she says, a grimace flashing across her face.

"The fu—" I stop myself from finishing that sentiment with the girls in the room.

"Believe me, it wasn't a hardship to lose that job. He was a creep, and I'm thankful to no longer be working for him. He felt like he was privileged since Daddy owned the company. Unfortunately for him, the hammer is about to come down, as a few of us reported him to HR and the police. If he doesn't get fired, the media backlash from a trial will sure do damage to his reputation. I just feel bad for his wife and kids, who will no doubt be caught in the middle of everything. Another one of my co-workers got him on video from her cell phone, propositioning her and holding a promotion over her head with his threats. He was vile and I'm glad I was only an employee there for the couple of months that I was."

"Well, damn. I'm glad you got out. You should have quit sooner and come here."

"I was scared to do that. I needed the job to pay my bills. I kept applying around town and nothing would come of my interviews. So, when he fired me, I took that as my sign that it was time to cut out and move on."

"Well, you're safe here. And without rent hanging over your head for a while, at least, hopefully you can get on your feet and find a good job," Jillian says.

"I sure hope so."

"Maybe you can check and see if the team office has any marketing positions open?" Jillian says to me. "Or over at the Eagles office?"

"Maybe. Only if you promise to stay away from the players. They tend to be a-holes," I warn.

"Derek," Jillian groans my name in a warning tone.

Riley bounces her eyes between the two of us as we have a stare down for a moment. "Something you two want to enlighten me on?" she finally asks, breaking the tension.

"Just helping to keep your brother in check. He wasn't too happy about me mentioning helping you find a nice guy to date. He likes to still think of you as a little girl he needs to protect. Forgets that you're all grown up and can take care of yourself. Are old enough to date and drink and do other adult things," Jillian says, glaring at me, daring me to disagree with her, then smiling at Riley when she's done.

"Ah. I was a little worried about that when I decided to move close to him. He's probably worse than Dad." She laughs.

"I remember when you went on your first date in high school. I thought your mom was going to kill your dad because of his antics," Jillian replies, reminiscing with my sister.

"Yeah, it wasn't fun at the time. Embarrassing as all get-out. But it wasn't completely unwarranted. I can't even tell you how many guys tried to date me or get close just because this one is my brother." She points at me. "They all wanted the chance to meet him or use the connection to try and get somewhere with baseball. It's one of the main reasons I never dated a player. I didn't need them using me for my connection to Derek."

"That pisses me off," I state. "Those fu- *guys*"—I once again have to stop myself from saying what I really want since the girls are in the room—"are lucky that I was already gone by the time you made it to high school. If I'd have still been around, you can bet your ass I wouldn't have allowed any of them near you."

"Okay, caveman, how about some lunch?" Riley says, defusing the conversation.

"We've got sandwich makings, or I can heat up the fajita leftovers from last night," Jillian says, standing to head for the kitchen.

"Whatever is easier for you," Riley says, following behind her, leaving me in the living room to grumble under my breath for another minute, where I stay with the girls until we're called to come eat.

TWENTY-TWO

JILLIAN

THE LAST FIVE WEEKS HAVE FLOWN BY AND TODAY Derek has to board a flight, as he's due for pitchers and catchers camp tomorrow. The offseason always flies by, and this one was no different. It's amazing we started the offseason with our divorce being finalized to being back together again before a new season started. I never thought we'd be in such a good place so quickly, but I'm glad we are.

"How are you feeling?" Derek asks as he sits down on the edge of the bed next to me. I've been puking my guts out for the last twenty-four plus hours. The girls were so kind to bring home a stomach bug from preschool, and after they both suffered through it, it also took me down. He's been so helpful while I've been dealing with nothing but puke over the last couple of days.

Riley has also stepped in to help when needed. It's been so nice having her around. Since Derek and I were in college and she was only twelve when we met, we've never really gotten to spend much time together other than family vacations and weeklong visits throughout the years. But, now that she lives here, we see her all the time and our relationship has really blossomed. The girls love having their Aunt Ry at their disposal, and we're all excited to be heading out to Arizona in two weeks, once Derek is well into the swing of camp.

"Ugh. I've been better. Even pregnancy nausea isn't this bad. I just hope you don't get sick."

"Drink this," he says, handing me a Gatorade. "You need the electrolytes. And if I do, then I do. They can do without me for a few days of camp, if that's the case."

"But you won't have anyone there to take care of you." I pout as I bring the drink to my lips. The smell of the drink hits my nose and my stomach rolls. I hand it back to Derek quickly, covering my mouth in the process. "Nope, can't do it," I tell him as I jump from the bed and run for the bathroom. I heave over the toilet and he comes in right behind me, holding my hair back as I empty my stomach once again into the toilet.

"I think you need to go to the doctor, babe. This is lasting longer than it did for the girls and appears to be much stronger for you. Why don't you let me make you an appointment?" he suggests as he helps me back into bed.

"Maybe. But you have to fly out in a few hours."

"I can change my flight. Take one tomorrow, if needed."

"Won't you get in trouble for not reporting on time?"

"You're more important. And so what if I miss day one? I know the drill. Day one is more for the rookies than anyone. Coach will understand if I tell him it's because of family."

"Okay, call and see if they can get me in," I concede.

He grabs his cell from his pocket, and after unlocking the screen, he taps a few times, then the ringing of the phone fills the room.

"Family Practice, how can I help you?" the receptionist

answers.

"Hello, this is Derek Smyth, I'm calling for my wife, Jillian. She's a patient of Dr. Lamore and needs to be seen. The sooner, the better, please."

"Dr. Lamore just had a cancelation on her schedule for eleven forty-five. Can you come then?" she asks.

Derek looks over at me and I nod my approval. I don't miss how he referred to me as his wife. Some days, it's easy to forget that, according to the government, we're no longer married. I know he's alluded to the fact he wants to fix that and get married again, make it legal once again, but that's a conversation for another time.

"We'll be there," he assures her.

"And what does Mrs. Smyth need to be seen for?"

"Our girls passed on their stomach bug to her, but it's lasting much longer than it did for them, plus, appears to be much worse for her. I'm worried she might be dehydrated at this point."

"I've got it noted. If needed, they can administer an IV to give her some fluids while she's here in the office."

"Thank you, we'll be in soon." He hangs up with the receptionist then turns to me. "I'll feel better leaving you knowing that you're going to be okay," he says before standing up. "I'm going to go make sure that Ry can stay here with the girls while I take you."

"Thank you," I croak out. Seeing that I only have about an hour until my appointment time, I find the energy to head for the shower. Maybe the hot water will help me feel better.

An hour and twenty minutes later, we're sitting in the exam room and I'm hooked up to an IV, getting pumped full of fluids as we wait for Dr. Lamore to return. She had some labs drawn to make sure I don't have anything more than the stomach bug the girls had, as she also agrees it shouldn't have lasted as long as it has with me.

"How are you feeling?" Derek asks, now that I've gotten half the bag of fluids in me.

"Better. The meds also helped with that." They gave me some anti-nausea meds in my IV to help with how queasy I've been.

"Good. The color is returning a bit to your cheeks. Maybe after we leave here, you'll actually be able to eat something and keep it down."

"Maybe. Just the thought of food makes my stomach roll. So, it will have to be something light, if I can even stomach it."

"Whatever you want, babe," he says, leaning over and kissing my forehead.

"How's it going in here?" Dr. Lamore asks as she pushes open the door.

"Good. No puking, so that's a good sign," I tell her.

"Well, good news. You don't have anything else, infection-wise, causing you to be sick, but there is something that is aiding to it. Congratulations, you're pregnant," she says, a smile plastered on her face.

"Did you say pregnant?" I ask in disbelief.

"I sure did." She pulls a portable ultrasound machine to the side of the exam table. "And looking at your bloodwork numbers, only a few weeks along. We can take a quick peek and get a look at the sac and give you an idea at a due date."

I look over at Derek and the look of complete joy that lights up his face is all I need to see. I took his conversation about knocking me up last month as a joke, not that I didn't think it was a possibility, since we used no protection and weren't careful about avoiding my fertile days.

She sets up the machine then steps out while I undress

from the waist down so she can do the vaginal ultrasound. She returns a few minutes later and after applying gel to the end of the probe, inserts it. Derek and I both look at the screen in amazement as she points out the tiniest flicker on the screen. The baby is measuring at five weeks exactly, which, if I count back, is probably the time of that morning against the bathroom wall. The same day he talked about us having another baby.

"The baby looks great right now. With being five weeks today, that gives you a due date of October fifteenth."

"Right in the middle of the playoffs," I muse, looking over at Derek.

He grabs my hand and brings it to his lips to kiss. "We'll make it work."

"Hopefully, between the Zofran and the fluids, you'll start feeling better and get over the stomach bug. I think it was being prolonged by the pregnancy and getting dehydrated. If you start feeling like you have been, call and we'll get you in right away, even if it's just with the nurse for some more fluids. You should be fine to wait until you're eight to ten weeks along to see your OBGYN, but I'd call and make an appointment with them to make sure they don't want to see you sooner. Do you still see Dr. Abbott?"

"I do," I confirm.

"Good, I'll send her a note to tell her about the pregnancy and to expect to see you in a few weeks. She'll be able to see the lab reports and ultrasound from today, as well."

"Thank you."

"Absolutely, my dear. Do you have any questions for me? I know this isn't your first pregnancy, but just wanted to make sure."

"Nothing that I can think of, thank you."

"Sure thing. Once you finish off this bag of fluids, we'll

get you unhooked and on your way. It shouldn't be more than another ten, maybe fifteen, minutes. Feel free to get dressed once I step out."

"Thank you," Derek tells her before she leaves the room as I get dressed as best as I can with an IV line hooked up.

"Can you believe it?" I ask Derek, still a little shocked as I get settled back on the table.

"Marry me? Again, please, Jillian," Derek says as he stands, boxing me in as an arm goes to each side of my body on the exam table. All I see when I look up at him is the love that shines in his eyes.

"Yes." It's the only answer I can give him as his lips crash against mine. "Germs," I try and say against his lips.

"I don't care about any fucking germs," he says against my lips. "I'll take every germ you can give me." He only pulls back when there's a knock at the door. The nurse peeks her head in and sees the bag of saline is now empty and I'm ready to be disconnected and sent home.

"Call if you have any more complications," she reiterates before we leave the room. Derek grabs my hand, linking my fingers with his as he leads me out to his truck. He's practically bouncing as we walk, with all his excitement.

"Chill out, honey," I tease him once we're in the truck.

"No can do," he states. "We're getting married again— and soon." He stares at me. "And I knocked you the fuck up. I'd say today is the best damn day. Well, minus all the puking you've had to do."

"Yeah," I say on a sigh. "I didn't think you were that serious about the whole 'knocking me up' speech last month."

"What can I say, when I put my sights on a home run, there's nothing stopping me from knocking one out of the park."

I laugh at his use of baseball references. "If you say so."

"Are you doubting my abilities, woman?" he asks as he pulls out of the parking lot.

"Nope," I tell him, popping the P.

He points toward my abdomen. "Didn't think so. Since I already proved that I can knock you up."

"I hope this pregnancy is just as easy as the girls' were," I muse.

"I'm looking forward to the second trimester, myself," he says, giving me a devilish grin as he bounces his eyebrows.

"You would." I laugh. "Are you still going to make your flight tonight?" I ask, noticing the time.

"I changed it to the six a.m. one. Already told Coach that I'll head straight to the field from the airport and he was fine with it."

"When did you do that?"

"I texted him before we left the house. Said that you were sick and I needed to take you to the doctor, and I wasn't sure if I'd be able to fly down tonight. Said to keep him informed. I also went ahead at that time and changed my flight, let him know, and he was also fine with that."

"Look at you, being all on top of everything."

He squeezes my fingers. "As I've said, I'm a changed man."

"I'm going to hold off on telling the girls about the baby for a little while," I tell him as we pull into the driveway. "I'll tell Riley when they aren't around and I don't care if you tell the guys, but I want to wait a week or two to tell the girls. They're going to be pestering us about when the baby will come for long enough, so the longer we can wait, the shorter the amount of time we have to deal with their relentless questions."

"You're the boss. I'll follow your lead."

We head inside and find Riley and the girls cleaning up from some lunch. The smell of food causes my stomach to growl, a nice change from rolling and running to the toilet as I've dealt with the last day.

"How's everything around here?" Derek asks his sister.

"All's well. We were going to walk down to the park after lunch. Run some of the returned energy out before naptime."

"Sounds like a perfect idea," he says, hugging both of our girls. I love watching him with them. He's such a good dad. I can't wait to see him with another little one in his arms. The man can melt panties just by himself, but you put an itty-bitty baby in his arms and poof, I'm a goner.

"How was the appointment?" Riley asks me.

"Good, I'll tell you about it later. Cliff notes are that I was dehydrated, and after some fluids and Zofran, I'm hopefully back on the mend."

"Okay. I look forward to the expanded version later then," she says before turning to the girls. "Go get your shoes on and we'll head to the park!"

"Yay!" both girls exclaim as they hop down from their seats and head for the shoe rack.

"Don't forget to potty first!" I call out to both of them, then glance over at Riley. "The park doesn't have any bathrooms, and it never fails; we get there and one of them has to go."

"Ah, good thinking. I've got lots to learn before I have kids of my own."

"I promise you, it will all come to you eventually. And you just have to remember that kids don't come with owners' manuals. You'll screw up with something, but thankfully, kids are resilient. They won't remember the time when you forget the diaper bag for that quick run to Target and end up needing to buy a new outfit for the both of you, along with a package of diapers and wipes to give both of you a wipe bath in the bathroom because of a diaper blowout mid-shopping trip.

"Nor will they remember the time you lose your shit because you're so exhausted from the lack of sleep that you just sit down in the middle of their nursery and cry right along with them when they're teething and it's three a.m., and you haven't slept since three the morning before, except a few ten-minute cat naps spread throughout the day."

I smile, thinking back on a few of my mishaps as a parent. "But I also promise you that it's the best job I've ever had and the best title I'll ever hold. The good times far outweigh the bad. I promise," I tell her, hoping I haven't scared her too much.

"Oh, I know. One little boy I used to babysit in high school used to blow out his diaper every single time I watched him. He loved his little jumper contraption, but the thing always caused that to happen."

"Ah yes, the girls did the same thing sometimes when we'd put them in theirs," I tell her.

"On that note, I'm going to get out of here with them. We'll be back in a little bit."

"Have fun," I call out as she ushers the girls to the door.

"What would you like to eat?" Derek asks me once they're gone.

"Maybe a grilled cheese?"

"Perfect, something I actually know how to make," he teases. I take a seat at the counter and watch as he pulls the items from the fridge and the bread from the cabinet. "So, how long do I have to wait until you'll marry me again?"

I shrug my shoulders at him as he places the sandwich

on the hot pan. "Um, I don't know. We don't need anything elaborate. But you're leaving in the morning and won't be back for a few weeks, so it will have to wait until at least then."

"I'll be back in six weeks. We can go down to the courthouse the next day and get it done."

"That will work."

"Damn straight, it will," he says, placing a plate in front of me with a perfectly grilled sandwich. He leans even further over and presses a chaste kiss against my lips before pulling back and making himself a couple sandwiches.

We move to relax on the couch once we finish up lunch. My stomach is handling the sandwich well, and hopefully that continues for the rest of the night. I'm finally starting to feel better now that I'm hydrated and have some food in me. As we sit here, watching TV, I try to wrap my mind around the fact that we're pregnant and having another baby. The thought brings tears to my eyes.

"What's wrong?" Derek asks.

"Nothing," I tell him, sniffling as I attempt to stop the tears.

"It's not nothing. Talk to me, baby," he says, rolling me over so I'm facing him.

"It just hit me that we're having another baby. They're good tears, I promise. I'm just shocked, overjoyed, scared, thinking what in the hell did we just get ourselves into. We're going to be outnumbered, Derek. How am I going to take care of *three* babies when you're gone?" I word vomit all over him, not holding back as my mind races with the questions and what-ifs.

"We'll figure it out as we go. And, the last time I checked, you are kind of Supermom. I'm sure you'll rock this 'mom of three' thing. It might be crazy, and hard at times, but we wouldn't have it any other way. If I'm not mistaken, didn't you tell me early on in our dating days that I'd better be okay with a house full of kids since you wanted at least four?"

"I might recall that conversation," I reply as he wipes the tears from my cheeks. "But I'm far from being Supermom. Do you know how many days we don't even change out of our PJ's until after lunchtime? Or how many nights I make them grilled cheese and soup because I don't feel like cooking a big meal?"

"Nothing is wrong with either of those scenarios. What do you remember most about your childhood? What your mom cooked each night? Or what time of day you got dressed? No, you remember the good times—the family trips, traditions, your favorite meal that she'd make for specific occasions. Those are the things that our kids will remember."

"I know, I just don't like the labels of being a Supermom or Instagram-ready. We already have so much pressure on us from every angle, the thought of being that perfect parent is just one that I can't handle being put on my shoulders, because I *will* fail at some point. I just always hope that it isn't when anyone is watching."

"Even if they are, I'd challenge them to tell me who is a perfect parent. No one, that's who. Everyone fucks up at some point or another. It's how one grows from that experience that shows their true colors and maturity."

"I'm pretty sure I'm the one that said those exact words to you, not long ago," I tell him, snuggling in closer as exhaustion hits me out of nowhere—thank you, first trimester tiredness mixed with being sick for the last day. I nod off in Derek's arms, the steady beat of his heart lulling me off to sleep.

"Sʜʜ... Mᴏᴍᴍʏ's ɴᴀᴘᴘɪɴɢ," I ʜᴇᴀʀ Dᴇʀᴇᴋ ᴛᴇʟʟ Penelope and Addison. "She needs to sleep to feel better." They quietly sit down on the floor next to the couch. I'm not fully awake, and still have my eyes closed, but I can sense they're close by. "How was the park?" he asks Riley, his voice whisper quiet.

"Good. We had the place to ourselves," she softly tells him. It sounds like she's sitting on the recliner a few feet away. "How's she doing?"

"Good. Has kept down her lunch and fell asleep maybe twenty minutes ago."

"Probably needed both the food and the sleep."

"That she does. I'm really glad that you'll be around to help her out while I'm gone. I hate that I have to leave tomorrow morning, but we knew the time was coming."

"You know I don't have any problem with helping out, it's the least I can do for everything that the two of you are doing for me."

I feel bad practically eavesdropping on their conversation, but I'll hopefully drift back into a deep sleep if I just stay here, still and with my eyes closed. I'm not ready for my nap to end just yet.

"I appreciate that," he tells her.

"Penny, Addison." Riley gently calls the girls' names to gather their attention. "Let's go potty and then go lay down for a nap. Aunt RyRy needs a nap. You wore me out!" I listen as they get up and follow her out of the room without one ounce of fight. I wish they'd do the same for me that easily. With the conversation stopped, the sound of Derek's heart beating lulls me back to sleep.

TWENTY-THREE

DEREK

I'VE BEEN IN ARIZONA AT TRAINING CAMP FOR ALMOST two weeks already. The first few days sucked being away from Jillian, Penelope, and Addison. That all changes today when they, along with my sister, fly in to spend the next three weeks down here with me. Jillian was able to find a nice house to rent on Airbnb for the time, so they'll have more room than just a hotel. With being here for that long, having a kitchen is a necessity, as is laundry and just space, in general.

Derek: Got everything ready to head to the airport?

Jillian: Just about. Ry is here and helping me. I swear, these girls have more crap to bring than your entire team does.

Derek: Just think what a third one is going to add to the mix.

Jillian: Don't remind me. Just be thankful I've saved most of the baby things. We'll hopefully only need to buy a few new things and just re-use everything else.

Derek: Baby things are the least of my worries today, babe. How are you feeling today? I'm hoping you're feeling good as I have grand plans for after the girls are sleeping tonight. :devilish grin:

Jillian: I'm feeling pretty good today so far. I swear, this baby must be a boy for how differently this pregnancy has been compared to the girls.

Derek: Maybe! We can find out in what, eleven weeks?

Jillian: More like thirteen. Sometimes they'll take a guess if they can get a good look that early, but the standard time is around twenty weeks. So, we've still got some time to go before we'll know.

Derek: What are you hoping for?

Jillian: Just a healthy baby. A girl would just fit into the fold so easy since that's all I know how to be the mom of, but a little brother would be pretty damn fun. What about you?

Derek: Same, babe. As long as he or she is healthy and looks like you is fine with me. I'll love them just as much as I love our big girls, hell, I already do, and all I've seen is the flicker of the heartbeat.

Jillian: Sorry to break up this serious conversation, but our ride just pulled up and I need to get the girls loaded up so we can head for the airport. I'll text you once we're boarded and on our way. See you later tonight. Love you.

Derek: Love you and be safe. I can't wait to see all of you. I've missed you all so much these past couple of weeks.

I slide my phone onto the shelf of my locker and head for the field. We're playing a mid-afternoon pre-season game against Texas and I'm starting. I hit the field and head straight for the pitcher's area to start warming up my arm. I pitch for ten minutes or so, throwing balls at the target. Once my arm starts to feel loose and warm, I move out and start pitching to JJ. He's joined me out here, dressed in his catcher's equipment.

"You feeling good today?" he asks, after I throw a dozen or so pitches at him.

"Yeah, why?"

"No reason, just making sure." He throws the ball back to me. I toss it down on the ground and move onto some stretching. The last thing I want to do is pull a muscle and hurt myself before the regular season starts.

JJ joins me on the side of the field as I work my way through my pre-game ritual. We've been doing this since our rookie season, when we first started playing together. Like nearly all sports, and athletes, we each have our own way of getting mentally prepared for the game, and this is just one of the many things we do. Once the game starts, not many people will talk to me between innings while I'm pitching. I don't want the distraction. Call me superstitious, but the more I can focus in on the game, the better I am at throwing strikes.

"What time is Jillian and the crew arriving?" he asks when we finish up stretching and move on to some wind sprints.

"Flight gets in just after six. She's picking up the rental at the airport and will drive over to the house. I just plan on going to the house once we can leave here. Depending on how long this game goes, I might even beat them there."

"You staying there tonight or coming back to the hotel?"

"I'll probably end up staying. With having tomorrow off, I'll be over there all day anyways, so I might as well just stay. That, and I haven't gotten laid in a few weeks. Time to change that."

"Pussy whipped," he says under his breath. "I've gotten laid every night I've been here," he adds, as if it's something to be proud of.

"Yeah, and how many names can you even remember?"

"Uhhh... maybe one? That is, if she even gave me her real name."

"That shit is going to get you in trouble one of these days. For all you know, you've got some kids running around out there."

"Shut your mouth," he says seriously, turning to look at me. "I might fuck around a lot, but I never go without protection."

"You do know that shit doesn't always work, right? Like, only ninety-nine-point-nine percent, or some shit like that."

"I'm aware, and thank my lucky stars I've never had a condom break on me, and so far, no one has showed up on my doorstep claiming I'm their baby daddy. Well, there was that one crazy chick a few years ago, but a simple paternity test proved her wrong."

"Just be careful, would you?" I warn him. "One of these days, you're not going to be so lucky. Or you're going to meet a woman and she's going to knock you on your ass, and you won't know what hit you."

"Once again, shut your mouth," he says, punctuating each word with a punch to my chest. I just laugh at his complete horror at the thought of kids or settling down.

"Enough about all that, we've got a ball game to win," I tell him as I take off for one last sprint.

After my warmup, I head back to the locker room and check my cell one last time for any messages from Jillian. They should be to the airport by now, but I resist calling her as she's probably busy trying to get everyone checked in and through security.

I HOLD THE BALL IN MY HAND, ROLLING IT AROUND, and feel the threads as they lace around the ball. I watch as JJ flashes me signals for the type of ball he wants me to throw. He signals for a fastball, and I shake my head, telling him no. Breaking ball is the next signal, and that one I like. I nod slightly, letting him know that's what to expect.

I stand to my full height, check my players, and wind up my arm. The ball seamlessly leaves my fingertips and does exactly what it's supposed to do. The batter swings and misses. The umpire calls the strike, and the batter is out. He's the sixth straight batter I've struck out. That doesn't happen often, but when it does, it's a great feeling. I pull my hat off and wipe the sweat that's gathered along my hairline before tugging my cap back on, then I run for the dugout and take my seat off to the side of everyone else. JJ is the only one to come close, and even he keeps his distance, giving me my space to keep myself in my own head. If I allow the distractions around me to get inside my head, my game will go to shit.

Our first baseman, Matt O'Riley, is up to bat first. He fouls the first pitch by a sliver of space off the third base line. Texas' pitcher must not like the signals his catcher is sending his way, as it takes them a good thirty seconds or so to decide what pitch to throw. Indecisiveness like that shows how immature and unsure the pitcher is of his own game.

He winds up his arm and releases the ball. Unfortunately for the pitcher, he read Matt completely wrong. Matt connects with the ball and sends it up and out of the park. Single home run, adding to our already cushy lead of eight to zero. The rest of the eighth inning goes by without any more runs; we strand one guy on second base when Texas is able to close out the inning. The ninth inning goes about the same, although I let one guy on base. Thankfully, he doesn't get past that point when we finish out the game. Although it's only the pre-season, it's still nice to get the win. The majority of our team are all returning players, but we've got a few new players who have to adjust to the way we do things.

As soon as the game is over, I head for the locker room. After talking with a few reporters about how I felt after pitching a full game today, I head for the showers. Jillian texted that they made it and she was just waiting for the rental car, then they'd be on their way to the house. I rush through my shower and as soon as Coach releases us, I head straight for my own rental car out in the players' parking lot.

I plug the address of the rental house into my GPS and pull out. The house is only about ten minutes or so away from here, so it's nice and close. It will be easy for me to go over and see them during my off time. I'm required to stay with the team for most of the preseason, but during my off time, you can be damn sure I'll be with my family this year.

TWENTY-FOUR
JILLIAN

I PULL INTO THE DRIVEWAY OF THE HOUSE WE'VE rented for the next two weeks and punch in the code for the gate. I love that we have that small added level of security. Not that I think any crazy fans will bother us, but you can never be too safe. It's one of the reasons I don't mind living in the gated community we do back in Indianapolis. Knowing we're not going to have random people driving by our house and taking pictures of the girls out playing is comforting.

Once the gate opens, I pull up to the house and park in front of the garage.

"I'm going to go in and open the garage. I'll be right back," I tell Riley and my girls.

"We'll be here," she replies from the passenger seat. She's been a godsend the last few weeks, helping me, as I've been exhausted and dealing with some morning sickness I never had to deal with for either girl.

I head up the steps and punch in the door code I was given. The instructions also said I'd find the garage door opener on the kitchen counter, so I head straight for that, finding it, along with a paper with some more details about the house and welcoming us for our stay. I find my way to the garage, open the door, then pull the rental car in. Riley hops out and helps me get the girls, then starts unloading the luggage.

"Don't feel like you have to get all of it. Derek can get the rest when he gets here," I tell her as I follow the girls in.

We go exploring, looking in each room to get the lay of the house. I drop the one bag I carried in of mine in the master bedroom, then take the girls down the hall and show them the room where they'll be sleeping. This house is perfect for us, as it has a room with two twin beds all set up for two little girls, the master for me and Derek when he can be here, and another junior master on the other side of the house for Riley to use. The backyard is a kid's oasis, with a large playground set and lots of open space to run and play.

The girls each take a turn laying down on the beds and pick what ones they each want. Thankfully, they don't want the same one, so no fights to referee over that. We head back up to the living room and my phone starts ringing. It's an unknown number, so I answer it to find it's the grocery delivery I'd set up, needing in the gate. I let them in, and once they've finished unloading, we get to work putting everything away.

Riley is right there helping me, just as she has been since Derek left. She was so ecstatic when I told her we were expecting again. I still haven't told Addison and Penelope about the baby yet, but they've sure been suspicious about why I've been so sick lately. But I've been able to brush it off with them so far. I only give it a few more weeks before I break down and tell them.

With all the groceries put away, I relax on the couch while the girls pull out some toys they found in one of the closets. Riley joins me as we wait for Derek to show up. I stop on a station recapping the games that took place today and we get to see a few small clips of Derek pitching. The commentators talk about how calm and confident he appeared out on the mound today. How strong his pitches were and speculate that if he can pitch like that for the majority of the season, the Lightning will go far this year. They've been a strong team for a few years now, making it into the postseason for the last three years, just falling short of making the finals and earning the ultimate trophy by winning the World Series.

Forty or so minutes go by and I hear a car door close outside, followed by the front door opening a moment later.

"Where are my girlies at?" Derek calls out as he enters. Addison and Penelope both pop up and run screeching toward the door.

"Daddy!" they yell as they leap into his arms. He picks them both up as if they're light as a feather.

"I missed you both so much," he tells them as he kisses their cheeks.

Penelope giggles and then rubs his short beard. "Daddy, that tickles."

"Like this?" he says, rubbing it against her neck, causing her to giggle harder.

"Y-yes," she says between fits of laughter. He turns and does the same to Addison, which gets her giggling just as hard as her sister.

"Where's Momma and Auntie RyRy?" he asks as he sets them down.

"On the couch, 'laxing," Penelope tells him. I love the way she mispronounces relaxing. Just one of her little quirks that reminds me she's still little and learning. He looks up and sees both Riley and I spread out on the two couches.

His smile grows when he spots me, our eyes connecting from across the room. Something shifts between us. Something I didn't realize was off-kilter, but just being back in the same room as him makes it all right.

He closes the distance to where I'm sprawled on the couch, he crouches down on his haunches next to me. He cups my cheek and slowly leans in, pressing his lips against mine. "I missed you," he says against my lips once he breaks the kiss, keeping it PG since we have an audience.

"Get a room, you two," Riley teases from the other couch.

"Get a room!" Addison copies her and we all break out laughing.

"Oops, forgot they repeat everything we say," Riley says once we've all had a good laugh.

"Could be worse," I reply.

"Have you guys had dinner yet?" Derek asks.

"We had a late snack on the plane, but nothing since we got here."

"Are you guys hungry? I can order something in, if you'd like."

"Groceries were already delivered, if you want something quick," I tell him. "But, if you're willing to wait, we can order something so none of us have to cook tonight. I'm exhausted and don't feel like it to be honest with you."

"How are you feeling? Flying go okay?" he asks me quietly.

"It was fine. I'm just tired. No puking today, so I take that as a win."

"Still having to take the meds the doctor gave you?"

"Yes, but I've been able to get down to just taking it in the morning to get me over the first part of the day. Once

I've gotten something in my stomach and started moving around, I'm usually pretty good."

"I'm glad to hear that." He drops another chaste kiss to my lips.

"How was the game?"

"It was really great. Felt really good out there." It was his first start for the preseason. With five starting pitchers on the team, they rotate through who starts.

"I saw a few highlights and you looked amazing."

"Hopefully I stay that way," he says, then stands up, and pulls out his cell phone, scrolling through it. "What do you ladies feel like eating tonight?"

"I'm open to almost anything," Riley answers him, and turns to me. "What do you think you can stomach?"

"I'm really craving a greasy cheeseburger," I tell them, and Derek just gives me a WTF look. He knows I don't usually eat cheeseburgers, but that's what sounds good to me at the moment.

He raises his eyebrows at me. "That's an interesting craving."

"What can I say, blame it on the..." I point at my abdomen and the itty-bitty baby growing inside of me.

"Duly noted." He snickers, scrolling until he finds a restaurant with a cheeseburger, and orders for all of us. "Food should be here in forty-five to sixty minutes," he says before dropping his phone on the end table.

"Before you get comfortable, I need you to do me a favor," I tell him, just before he sits down on the couch.

"What's that?"

"Can you bring in the rest of the luggage, please?" I look up at him, batting my eyelashes.

"Sure." He laughs at me, bending over and dropping a

kiss to my lips. "I'll collect payment later," he says so only I can hear.

He takes off for the garage and quickly brings in the suitcases, taking them back to the bedrooms, then joins us in the living room. The girls have gone back to playing with the toys they found, and I get sucked into an episode of some cooking competition on TV.

"I don't know how these people can be so creative with their designs," I say to Riley when they show off the work of one of the bakers.

"Right. It's like a masterpiece, and all someone is going to do is cut into it and eat it. I couldn't imagine putting that much time into a cake," she muses.

"And they're hella expensive. I don't even want to tell you how much I've paid for the girls' cakes when I've done the custom ones."

"I bet."

Derek sits down on the couch, picking my feet up and placing them in his lap once he's seated. He starts rubbing them, digging his thumbs into the arches. My eyes nearly roll back in my head as he works the tight muscles over.

"How's that feel?" he asks after a few minutes.

"Amazing. You might just put me to sleep if you keep it up."

"Do you need to go in and lay down?" he asks, concerned.

"Nope, if I lay down now, I'll be down for the night. I'll just go to bed shortly after the girls do."

We're interrupted by the buzzer going off, alerting us to someone trying to get in the gate. Derek takes care of letting the delivery guy in and goes to wait for him by the front door.

"Holy shit. You're Derek Smyth," the kid exclaims when he reaches the front door.

"That I am," he confirms. I watch the kid look at him with such starstruck eyes as he hands over the bags of food. I walk over and stand next to Derek.

"Do you have a cell phone? I can take a picture of the two of you," I offer, and the kid looks like he just won the lottery at my offer.

"Of course!" He starts patting all his pockets until he finds his phone tucked in one of his back ones. He pulls it out and opens up the camera. Derek sets the bags of food down on a small entryway table and stands out on the stoop to pose for a picture with the young man. I snap a couple pictures to make sure he has a good one to show off to his friends and family. "My buddies are going to be so jealous," he exclaims as he looks at the pictures.

"Do you play ball?" Derek asks him.

"Just a few years of Little League. I wasn't good enough to go further than that. My mom couldn't afford the year-round leagues or the travel teams," he says, shrugging his shoulders.

"That's okay, my man," Derek tells him, clapping him on the shoulder. "I'm sure there's something else you're destined to do and once you find it, you'll know it."

"Thanks," he replies. "I'd better go, I've got more deliveries to make. Have a good rest of your evening."

"Thanks, you too. Hold up for one second," Derek tells him as he pulls his wallet out. He takes some cash and hands it over to the kid. "An extra tip. Go do something nice for your mom."

"Thank you so much." The kid pockets the cash and almost stumbles off the stairs as he turns quickly to head down to his car. "I'll surprise her this weekend," he calls out before sliding into the driver's seat and closing his door.

"His answer was honest and not rehearsed. It's the least I could do for the kid," he says, shrugging his shoulders as he grabs the bags of food and heads for the kitchen.

I watch him as he walks, a smile on my face. He's always been a softie, helping people in need now that he can afford to.

TWENTY-FIVE

DEREK

I GET ALL THE FOOD PULLED OUT OF THE BAGS AND FIND some plates to use from one of the cabinets. The owners are definitely prepared, as they also had kid-friendly plates and utensils for the girls to use.

"Dinner's ready," I call out, and Addison and Penelope come running in.

"Go wash up," Jillian reminds the girls and they turn around. "The bathroom is just around the corner," she adds, realizing they're confused on where the bathroom is. She follows them in and helps them get all washed up before they return to the table and take their seats. I set the plates, along with cups, in front of them with milk from the fridge.

"Thanks, D," Riley tells me as she accepts the plate with her food on it. She lifts up onto her toes and places a kiss on my cheek before finding a seat of her own at the table.

"You're welcome. It's the least I can do for all your help," I reply before taking a seat between Addison and Penelope.

We've only been eating for a few minutes when Penelope looks over at Jillian. "Mommy, I don't feel good." We both turn our heads at the same time and see her face swelling.

"Shit!" Jillian jumps up from her seat. "Call an ambulance now!" she yells as she takes off down the hall. She comes running back in a few seconds later, her purse in hand as she digs out Penelope's EpiPen case. Thank God Riley was here, as she followed Jillian's instructions and called 911 while I froze and watched as my little girl swelled with hives and start gagging.

"Lay her on the floor, Derek!" Jillian instructs as she opens the EpiPen case. I do as she says, and Jillian injects the medicine into her thigh. As soon as the needle pierces her skin, Penelope screams out and starts crying between gags.

"What did she eat?" I ask, dumbfounded. "I promise I checked the allergy menu before I ordered her food."

A few seconds later, I hear the sirens outside. Riley must have taken care of letting them in the gate because, before I know it, two paramedics are entering the house, followed by some firemen, who all surround us. Jill explains what happened, and that we've already administered a round of Epi to her. They hook her up to a monitor and tell Jill she can sit on the stretcher first, then place Penelope in her lap before they strap both of them in.

"You can follow us to the hospital, Mr. Smyth," one of the paramedics tells me, and it snaps me out of my shock.

"Thank you," I reply, then turn to my sister.

"You go, I'll keep Addison here. Call or text me when you have any news," she says, then pushes me out the door, handing me my cell phone and keys.

I follow the ambulance as we make the short drive to the nearest hospital, where I aimlessly park and find the entrance for the emergency room. I walk straight up to the registration desk, waiting not so patiently for someone to help me.

"My daughter was just brought in by ambulance with an allergic reaction. Penelope Smyth," I tell the lady behind the desk.

"Just a moment, sir." She types something into her computer. "She's in Treatment Bay Five. Go through that door and down the hall. It will be on your left," she says as I hear the buzz of the door next to me opening.

I follow her directions and run down the hall, skidding to a stop when I find the exam room. When I enter, I find a nurse and doctor assessing her. They've removed her clothes and have monitors stuck to her chest and abdomen, as well as an IV inserted into her arm. She's clinging to Jillian, tears streaming down her cheeks.

"Penny!" I gasp under my breath. Jillian looks at me, the worry evident in her expression.

"Do you know what she was exposed to?" the doctor asks Jillian.

"I don't know for sure, but my guess is, the restaurant we ordered from uses peanut oil for their fries."

"If it was that, do you know how many fries she ingested?"

"Just a couple. We'd only been eating for two minutes tops when she reacted."

"Okay," the doctor says as he watches the monitor. Every inch of her body is covered in hives, so many that it almost appears as if her hives have hives. I've never seen something so bad. "Her vitals are good and I see no distress with her breathing. I'd like to monitor her for the next five or six hours to make sure she doesn't have any rebound reactions. My guess is she was able to vomit out everything she ingested. We've already pushed some steroids in her IV, along with the saline, so if she starts to get sleepy, that's why, and it's okay if she falls asleep."

I shake his hand. "Thank you, doctor."

"You're welcome," he tells me, then turns to Jill. "Your quick thinking definitely helped curb her reaction, and who knows, might have saved her life had it gotten bad enough to affect her airway."

"We got lucky, that's for sure," I interject.

I move the extra chair closer to the side of the bed and take a seat on it. I grab Jillian's hand, lacing her fingers with my own. I don't know what I would have done had something worse happened to Penelope, and I'm mentally kicking my own ass, since I'm the one who ordered the food and gave it to her. How could I be so careless? Just to be sure I didn't miss something, I pull up the restaurant's allergy menu and double check it once more. It clearly states they use canola oil in their fryers, so she should have been safe.

"I'm going to call the restaurant and find out what went wrong," I tell Jillian. I'm pissed now, and someone needs to answer for what happened.

I tap the button to call and it feels like it rings forever before someone finally answers.

"I need to speak with a manager immediately," I firmly tell the person on the other end.

"One moment, please," they state before placing me on hold. It takes probably thirty seconds for someone to pick up the line, which feels like thirty minutes, thanks to how shot my nerves are at the moment.

"This is Dave, how can I help you?"

"Hi, Dave, this is Derek Smyth and I placed an order for my family a little more than an hour ago, after reading over your restaurant's allergy menu to make sure it was safe for my daughter. I need some answers, as we're currently sitting in the emergency room after she reacted to something within a few bites. My wife thinks it might have been the oil you fry fries in. According to the website, you use canola. Is that still true?" I ask, as calmly as possible.

"I'm sorry to hear that your little girl is in the hospital. We typically use canola oil, but our supplier had a shortage and had to send us peanut oil."

"You might want to place a notice to your customers about that change. It almost killed my little girl. Now, I can go to the media about this, or you can agree to warn other customers about the change until you switch back. Your company will also agree to cover any and all expenses we incur due to this ordeal. I don't like to use my status as a means for media coverage, but I will if need be," I tell him, with no remorse in my voice. He must take me seriously and know I'm not joking around with my threats.

"Of course, sir. Is there an email I can send our office contact information to, for you to forward any bills that need reimbursed? I'll also make up some notice signs and have our servers inform customers of the change with each new table."

I give him my manager's email address and tell him additional communications may come from their office. I don't need this guy telling me one thing and then going against his word later on.

"You might check with your website people to also make note of the change on your website and within the ordering apps, as that is how we ordered."

"Thank you for the suggestion, I'll pass that information on, as well," he assures me.

"Someone from my management team will follow up

within the next few days to make sure things are in order," I reply before we disconnect the call.

"I figured it was the oil," Jillian tells me a few seconds later. "So many places don't realize just how deadly it can be to change something out like that without telling people about the change. Hopefully they'll learn their lesson from this."

"I just hope it didn't happen to anyone else."

"Me too."

Just then, Penelope stirs in her arms.

"Do you need me to take over?"

"Yes, I need to use the bathroom," she says, and I stand and pick Penny up from her lap. I carefully place her against my chest, her head resting on my shoulder, then help Jillian stand from the bed. Once she's out of the room, I get as comfortable as I can on the bed, adjust Penelope in my lap, and pull out my phone.

> **Derek:** We're here and being monitored for a while. They gave her some steroids and fluids, and her hives are finally starting to recede. Thankfully, it never affected her airway. I called the restaurant and tore into them after they confirmed they switched types of oil without telling their customers.

> **Riley:** Holy crap. I'm glad she's doing okay. How are you and Jillian holding up? Need me to bring you anything?

> **Derek:** We'll be fine. Just stay there with Addison. How is she doing?

Riley: I think she was in shock. She cried for a bit after you guys left, but I was able to calm her down. Got her to finish her dinner and we're watching a movie now together in my bed. I don't think she's going to last much longer before she passes out.

Derek: Thanks for keeping her. We really appreciate it. Also, thanks for not freezing up like I did when Jillian told us to call 911.

Riley: Don't mention it.

I drop my cell on the bed when Jillian comes back in the room. She looks exhausted, yet beautiful all at the same time.

"I was just updating Riley and checking in on Addison," I tell her as she leans over the bed and pushes Penelope's hair from her face, tucking it behind her ear.

"And, how is she?"

"She said she was scared right after we left, but that she's almost asleep. Ry was cuddling with her on her bed and they were watching a movie together."

"I'm sure the excitement of the ambulance and fire truck scared her. Plus, how scared we were when everything was going on."

I nod my head in agreement. I know how scared *I* was, and I'm an adult. I can't even imagine what it was like for her to see that happen to her sister, and then for both Jillian and I to disappear. I lay my head back on the pillow behind me and let what happened sink in. Tears prick my eyes as it all hits me once again.

I stop holding the emotion back. If I can't be vulnerable

in front of Jillian, then who can I be. She's just as much my rock as I am hers.

"Derek." Her sweet voice fills my head as I start to sob. I pull Penelope into a tighter embrace, remembering to be careful of the monitors and her IV line. "She's going to be okay," she says, trying to comfort me.

"I could have killed her," I finally grit out. "What kind of father does that?"

"Honey, this isn't your fault." She tries to soothe me.

"I know it wasn't, but that doesn't make me feel less guilty or scared about it happening again. What would I have done if you weren't there to spring into action when I froze? Would things have turned out differently? Would I have known to Epi her and call for an ambulance?"

"You can't Monday-morning quarterback the situation. Now you've seen firsthand what a reaction can look like and will know what to do if it ever happens again. Always Epi and call for an ambulance. That's our action plan," she tells me.

"Sorry to interrupt," a nurse says as she pushes into the room. "I just need to switch out Miss Penelope's fluids real quick."

"Of course." Jillian sits down in the chair next to the bed and I watch as the nurse expertly changes out the empty bag of saline for a new one.

"Her vitals are looking wonderful. No signs of rebound reactions at this point. The doctor said that if that continues while this bag of fluids is pushed, then we can let you guys go home. She will need to be on steroids for the next few days. Do you want me to send those to a pharmacy or have the hospital pharmacy fill them for you?"

"The hospital pharmacy is perfect. I don't even know

where a pharmacy is located. We just flew in earlier today," Jillian tells her.

"I hope your visit gets better," the nurse replies. "I'll get those prescriptions sent down and they'll send them up to us when ready."

"Thank you," we both call out to the nurse as she leaves the room.

TWENTY-SIX

JILLIAN

It's late by the time we make it back to the house. Riley and Addison are sound asleep in Riley's bed when I peek in to check on them. I stand in the doorway for a few seconds, looking at my oldest. I can't believe she's going to be five soon. Off to kindergarten in the fall. My hand falls to my abdomen and cradles my ever-so-small bump that has started to form. Most people would miss it or think I'd just eaten a large meal, but I've noticed in the last week it's sticking around. With this being my third pregnancy, my body knows what to do and is adjusting early on.

"She didn't even flinch when I put her down," Derek whispers in my ear as he comes up behind me, wrapping his arm around my waist and pulling me against him.

"I didn't think she would. The steroids they gave her will make her really sleepy," I tell him as I lay my head back on his chest. The exhaustion of flying here today, coupled with our visit to the emergency room, the time difference, and it being the middle of the night, I'm just about dead on my feet.

"Let's get you off to bed," he suggests, tugging on me to follow him down the hall and into the master bedroom.

We both go about our business of getting ready for bed. I notice the monitor on the nightstand and realize Riley must have unpacked the girls' things and gotten it set up for me. I slip out of our room and into the girls' room, finding the monitor in here already on. I look over Penelope one last time, stopping to tuck her hair behind her ear and out of her face. She looks so peaceful. I watch her breathe—normally, thank God—for a few breaths before I slip out of her room and back into mine.

"She doing okay?" Derek asks as he walks out of the bathroom. He's stripped down to his boxer briefs already.

"Yeah, I was mainly checking to make sure the monitor was turned on. Riley must have unpacked it for me."

"I saw that in there and wondered if it was ours or was provided by the owners."

"After tonight's events, I'm glad I thought to pack it. It will help me sleep better knowing I can hear her if she needs us during the night."

I watch as Derek stops at the edge of the bed and pulls back the comforter and sheet. He sets his phone and watch on their chargers, then slips into bed. "Come join me. You need to get some sleep."

I shake my head, the exhaustion causing me to zone out slightly. "I'll be right there," I tell him before disappearing into the bathroom. I quickly go through my nighttime routine, then join him in bed.

"In the morning, I want you to sleep in. I'll get up with the girls when they get up," he says once I'm settled in bed, my head resting in the crook of his arm. Our legs are tangled together, and my right hand rests on his chest.

"Okay." Just then, a yawn escapes. "You won't hear any

arguments from me about that," I tell him before drifting off to sleep.

I WAKE UP TO AN EMPTY BED. I ROLL OVER, FEELING the bed where Derek once slept next to me, and find the sheets cold, which tells me he's been up for a while. The fullness of my bladder tells me it must be late, so I roll over and slide out of this amazing bed. I swear, I haven't slept that good in a long-ass time. After using the bathroom and quickly brushing my teeth to rid me of my horrible morning breath, I head out to find everyone. When I open the bedroom door, I have to blink my eyes a few times as the sunlight hits them and is bright. The bedroom had blackout shades that do a fantastic job of keeping the light out.

I hear giggling coming from down the hall, so I walk that way. I find the girls playing in the living room, a Disney movie on the TV for them they aren't really paying attention to. Looking at Penelope, you'd never have guessed we spent most of the night at the hospital with her.

"Mommy!" Addison calls out when she sees me. "You're awake!" She runs over and throws her arms around my torso.

"I am. Did you sleep good with Auntie RyRy?" I ask, leaning down to kiss the top of her head.

"Yes. She let me sleep with her because I was scared."

"I know, baby," I tell her, dropping down to my haunches so I'm more at her eye level. "But sissy is okay, the doctors gave her medicine that helped her."

"RyRy put her food in the trash."

"I know, sweetie. Her food made her very sick. Have you had breakfast yet?"

"Yes, Daddy made us breakfast."

I can hear Riley and Derek talking from the kitchen. Addison returns to where her sister is playing, and I go find the adults.

"Morning, Sleeping Beauty," Derek greets me as I enter the kitchen and walk into his open arms. "How'd you sleep?"

He hands me his cup of coffee and I hold it up under my nose, taking a deep breath before I take a large sip of it. The warmth of the liquid warms me from the inside out. The smell and caffeine give me a jolt, helping me to wake up all the way.

"Thank you, I feel great. I slept like the dead. What time is it anyway?" I ask, looking around for a clock.

"Almost eleven," Riley pipes up.

"Eleven! Holy crap, I haven't slept in this late in forever."

"Well, you needed it," Derek assures me. "You had a long, stressful day yesterday."

"I won't argue with you there," I tell him as I finish off the cup of coffee.

"What's the plan for today?" Riley asks.

"I don't really have one, and if I did, I think that it would be shot. Is there something you wanted to go do?" I ask her.

"Nothing specific. I might need to drop by the store for a few things, but nothing that's an emergency."

"If you want to go, you're welcome to take the rental. I made sure that you were listed as a driver."

"Thanks, I might just do that in a little bit," she says as she slides off the bar stool. "I think I'm going to go shower and get dressed for the day."

Derek and I slip into a comfortable silence as I stand in

his embrace, empty coffee cup in my hand. I set it on the counter and attempt to reach for the pot that is just out of my reach. He takes pity on me and grabs it, then refills the cup.

"What time do you need to go today?" I ask, not really loving the idea he has to leave at some point.

"I'm not due back until tomorrow, mid-morning, so I'm all yours until then," he says, kissing the crown of my head.

"Okay. How has Penny been this morning? Any signs of a possible rebound reaction?"

"She's been her normal self since she got up. Slept until about eight thirty. I made them both some breakfast shortly after, and we've been just hanging out since."

"Thank you."

"You don't have to thank me for taking care of our girls."

"I know I don't, but you're also the one in the middle of training camp. You're the one who probably needs extra sleep, but here I am, the one getting it."

"Stop that. You need your sleep, you're growing another human, remember?" he chides. "I can deal with one night's lack of sleep. You shouldn't have to deal with it. Simple as that."

"I like this side of you," I tell him, pushing up on my toes to press my lips to his.

"Mhmmm..." He moans against my lips. "And I like this side of you," he says, nipping at my lips. "How about we find you something to eat, then take the girls out back and let them play while we relax in the shade?"

"That sounds perfect. I'm starving," I tell him. My stomach has been grumbling for a while. I rummage through the fridge before settling on some Greek yogurt for now. With it being almost lunchtime, I don't want to overdo it and then be off for the rest of the day.

Once outside, Derek helps me pull the lounge chairs out and place them in the shade, then hands me a bottle of water once I'm seated. I snagged my kindle before we came out so I can continue reading my current book. The girls took off for the play structure as soon as they came out here, and we're sitting so we can see them, no matter where they are.

"Do you want to bring the girls down to the game tomorrow?" Derek asks after awhile. I place my kindle down and look over at him.

"Sure, what time is the game at?"

"It's a noon start time," he tells me, his eyes still on the girls as they play. If he's anything, it's an overprotective father, and after last night's incident, I think his overprotectiveness is on high-alert.

"That will work. They might be tired come bedtime without a nap, but that isn't the end of the world. Plus, they always have fun going to games. Just too bad that we won't get to see you pitch tomorrow."

"If you come a bit early, I'll take them down on the field and let them throw the ball around."

"What time do you want us to arrive then?"

"Maybe around eleven," he suggests.

"Okay."

"I'll leave tickets at will call for you."

"Sounds like a plan."

"Hey, are you guys ready for some lunch?" Riley asks as she joins us.

"Maybe in a little bit. Did you already go and come back?" I ask, looking down at the time.

"Yep. I only needed a few things."

"Do you want to come to the game with us tomorrow?" I ask her before I forget.

"Sure!"

"That won't be a problem?" I ask Derek.

"Nope. I can get as many tickets as I want."

"I'm going to head back inside. Just holler at me when you're ready for some lunch, and I'll make some sandwiches and bring them out for everyone," Riley says before she turns for the door.

"Thank you," I call out after her.

I roll on my side, facing Derek as I turn back to reading my book. I'm lost in a chapter when I feel his hand slide across my belly, resting right over my little baby bump. "You're showing already," he says, astonished.

"I am. Not a lot, but it's definitely attempting to pop out. Third baby and all, my muscles are looser and know what to do by now."

"Can you believe it, babe. We're going to have another one!" The excitement that laces his voice just about brings me to tears. Knowing this surprise baby is already so loved and, while he or she shocked us with the timing, is very much wanted.

"I know. Some days, I still have to wrap my mind around it, but I knew deep down in my heart that our family wasn't complete with just two kids. I've always wanted a houseful, and I feel like that's an actual possibility now," I tell him as he entwines our fingers. He leans closer and brings his lips to mine.

"I love you," he whispers, and I feel his words down to my soul.

"I love you, too."

"I can't tell you how much I love hearing those words come from your lips. I worried I'd never hear them from you again," he tells me somberly.

"What's in the past is in the past. Let's look toward the future, okay?"

"Okay," he agrees as he presses another kiss to my lips.

"Mommy, can we have lunch?" Penelope asks, interrupting our moment.

"Yes, go run inside and tell Aunt RyRy that you're hungry. She said she'd make some sandwiches."

"Okay," she says in her sing-song voice, then takes off skipping to the back door.

"When did she get so damn big?" Derek asks as he watches her disappear inside.

"I swear, she's gone from a baby to a big girl in the past six months."

"She sure has."

"I think the no diapers or pull-ups mess really made her seem grown up," I state, then groan. "Ugh, diapers again."

Derek busts out laughing. "Weren't you just the one talking about having a house full of kids?"

"Yes," I whine. "I'm allowed to want a house full of kids but not want the diapers to go along with them."

"How about this?" He pauses to take a drink of his water. "We'll have as many babies as you want, and I'll help change as many of the diapers as I can when I'm home. Hell, hire a nanny to help you with diapers for when I'm not home, for all I care. I just want you happy."

"Well, aren't you just the sweetest," I tease. "And don't think you can trick me with the whole 'I'll change all the diapers when I'm home' line. I've heard that before." I roll my eyes at him. "You've weaseled your way out of way too many diaper changes with the girls, I won't fall for that again."

He has the audacity to give me a "who me" look while sporting a shit-eating grin.

"I'm on to you, mister."

"You can be *on* me anytime you want," he says, dropping his voice and raising his eyebrows at me.

I laugh out loud and smack his chest at the same time. "Stop it."

"What's so funny?" Addison asks as she pushes herself between our two chairs. Derek slips his hands under her armpits and pulls her onto his lap.

"Just something I was telling Mommy," he says, winking at me from over the top of her head.

"Guess what, Addy?" I say, grabbing her attention.

"What?"

"Tomorrow, Daddy's team is playing and we're going to go watch them!"

"Yay!" She starts to cheer. "Daddy, are you throwing the ball?" She's started to understand a little how the game is played, and that Derek doesn't always play.

"Not tomorrow. I played in yesterday's game," he tells her. "But, you, Penny, Mom, and Aunt Ry are going to come early, and I'll throw the ball with you before the game starts."

"Yes!" she says as she throws her arms around his neck. "I love you, Daddy."

Her words have my heart melting yet again.

"I love you, too, sweetheart."

TWENTY-SEVEN

DEREK

The past month has flown by. Training camp went about as it usually does. We got back home last night, and have two days until opening day. With today off, it's the perfect day for Jillian and I to head down to the courthouse to get married once again.

Coming home to her last night was everything. I never want to think about not coming home to her and our kids again.

"Morning, beautiful," I whisper in her ear after I roll over and pull her against me, her back flush to my front. My hand slides around her hip and rests against her now noticeable baby bump. I was shocked at how much her body changed in the few weeks we were apart after they returned from their time in Arizona. It feels like that was months ago, when it was really just a matter of weeks.

When she left, she had the smallest of bumps, but now it's not something she can hide easily. Everything on her has changed, and I'm loving it. She's always been beautiful to me, and pregnancy looks really good on her. I know she doesn't feel that way sometimes, but I'm here to make sure she believes me when I tell her.

"Morning," she says, still half asleep. I slip my fingers a little lower and past the elastic of her panties, circling a fingertip around her clit. "Mhmmm." She moans and presses her ass against my already hard cock.

"You ready to make it official once again, Mrs. Smyth?" I whisper as I plunge two fingers into her.

"Yes," she pants, and I roll her over onto her back. I slip down her body, gently dropping kisses against her skin. I remove my fingers and tug her panties down her legs, tossing them over my shoulder once I've cleared her feet. I drop down and bring my lips to her inner thighs, and I can feel her legs start to shake as I move closer to her center. When I reach the apex of her thighs, I run the top of my nose up her slit, following it with my tongue. I swirl my tongue around her clit before sucking it between my lips. "Derek!" She gasps my name as I slide two fingers back inside.

"Yes, baby," I say against her pussy. "Come for me."

I flick her clit with my tongue as my fingers work her from the inside. I feel her start to flutter around my fingers, so I curl them just slightly, hitting her g-spot, and suck hard on her clit. Her body goes rigid as she screams my name again. When she starts to go languid, I release her clit and slow my fingers, eventually pulling them from her sated body.

I kiss her hip bone, then along her bump, as I push her sleep tank up with my nose until I reach her luscious breasts. I know they're tender, as she's complained about it a few times the last couple of weeks, so I'm gentle when I lap at her nipples. I let her tank fall back down as I bring my body up, resting back against my pillow while she remains sated next to me. It takes her a few minutes to open her eyes and look over at me.

"Ready to marry me today?" I ask.

"After that, hell yes," she says, a hint of amusement lacing her voice.

"Admit it. You're only marrying me for my orgasm abilities," I tease.

"You are an expert in that department," she says, stroking my ego just a bit.

"Tell me something I don't already know."

"Don't get cocky now," she chides.

"I'll show you *cocky*," I tell her as I grab her hand and wrap it around my hard shaft.

"I'm sure you will, but hold that thought. This baby is already pressing on my bladder." She rolls out of bed and heads for the bathroom, returning only a few minutes later. She stops at the edge of the bed and pulls her sleep tank off, then slides in beside me, naked.

"Lay on your side," I tell her, then align my body with hers. I slip her top leg over mine and rub my cock along her entrance. "I can't wait to make you mine again today." I slip inside her, making slow, calculated thrusts. I'm in no rush. I've got all morning to make love to her. To make this moment and morning last.

"Derek." She moans my name. "I need more."

I slip my hand around and find her clit. It's swollen and sensitive.

"That's it, baby," I whisper into her ear. "Find your release. Come all over my cock. Make me come. Take what you need from me."

I grunt as I continue my steady, yet slow, thrusts. Most times, it feels like it's all about the speed and quick release, but there's something so sensual about this slowness, and the intimacy it brings to slowly build each other up until we find our mutual release.

"I'm close," I warn her. "Are you?"

Her only response is a nod of her head as she moans. Her finger joins mine as she shows me exactly how she needs to be touched. I feel the tingle travel down my spine and settle in my balls before I fall over the edge.

"Fuck, Jillian," I grunt as I empty into her. I thrust one last time, feeling as her body does the same and comes with me. We both still, and I hold her while we both bask in the endorphins flowing through our bodies in this moment.

"That was…" she starts to say, then trails off.

"Perfect," I answer for her.

"Yeah, we'll go with perfect," she agrees as I slip out of her and grab a washcloth I'd stashed on the nightstand to help clean up.

"What time do we need to leave for our appointment at the courthouse?" I ask a few minutes later. She's resting with her head on my chest while we savor the feelings from our love making.

"Around eleven. Our appointment is at noon, but we need to check in by eleven forty-five."

"Sounds good. And Riley is coming over to be with the girls?"

"Yes, she was going to be here by ten, if not earlier."

"Okay. I guess that means that I need to get up and get showered," I say, tapping her hip where my hand rests.

"If you must," she replies, attempting to burrow in closer to me.

"We must. That, and the girls are going to be up soon, if they aren't already. Someone's got to make them some breakfast."

"And that someone is going to be you?"

"Of course. You relax while I shower, then the bathroom is all yours to get ready for today. I'll take care of the girls," I assure her. I drop one last kiss to her forehead, then slip out of bed and head for the shower.

I STAND INSIDE A COURTROOM, NOT MUCH DIFFERENT than the one I sat in a few months ago. The feeling I had that day of complete dread is thankfully so very different than the hope and love I feel today. Jillian stands at my side, our fingers laced together as we wait to be called up by the judge.

"You ready?" I whisper so only Jillian can hear me. There are a few other couples all waiting for their names to be called.

"Yes, you?" She looks up at me with a smile tugging at the corners of her lips.

"Absolutely," I assure her. "Nowhere else I'd rather be."

"Smyth," someone calls out and we turn and head for the front.

"That's us," I tell the man when we reach him.

"Right this way." He gestures and we follow him into another room.

"Good afternoon." We're greeted by the judge, who proceeds to tell us how everything will go today. Neither one of us wanted the fanfare of a traditional wedding. We've already done one of those and didn't need to go through all of that again just to reverse our divorce from a few months ago.

Thirty minutes later, we walk out of the courthouse, hand in hand, with a piece of paper that legally binds us back together as husband and wife.

"Where to now, wife?" I ask Jillian as I sweep her into my arms and bring my lips to hers.

"Home, husband." She giggles as my lips move to her neck, my facial hair tickling her skin.

We head home and are surprised to find both sets of our parents there with the girls and Riley.

"Mom, Dad!" Jillian exclaims as she hugs both of her parents. "What are you doing here?"

"We couldn't miss your special day!" her mom says, wiping at a tear sliding down her cheek.

"You didn't have to come all the way here just for today."

"I know we didn't, but we thought that it would be nice to see everyone, plus, Dad wanted to be here for opening day."

"It's so good to see you," Jillian concedes, pulling her mom into another hug.

Our afternoon is filled with our families surrounding us and celebrating the fact that we found our way back to one another. I may have struck out once with the love of my life, but thankfully, I fought my way back and threw one last perfect pitch to win her back. That's not something I'll ever take for granted.

I STEP INTO THE LOCKER ROOM TWO DAYS LATER, feeling like my best season is on the horizon. My entire family is in the stands today to watch as we start the season off on our field.

"You feeling good?" JJ asks me as I tie my cleats.

"Better than ever. You ready?" I reply as I toss a ball at him.

"I was born ready, fucker." He tosses the ball back at me as we make our way out of the locker room and into the dugout. As we hit the field, I look up and make eye contact with Jillian. I kiss my fingertips and raise them up in her direction, and she does the same. We started this tradition way back in my college days. JJ and I begin our routine as we both get ready for the opening pitch. With it being opening day, we have all the pomp and circumstance to go along with that, since our game is being nationally televised.

By the time I finally take the mound, my mind is calm, my arm is warmed up, and I'm ready to start this season off with a win.

I strike out the first two batters with my first six pitches. That doesn't happen very often; someone usually hits a foul ball, but not tonight. Tonight, I'm damn well almost perfect with my pitches, but I don't read too much into it, as I don't want to throw off my focus. I just feel the ball, read the batters, and throw the balls JJ signals me to throw. By the eighth inning, I start to think about the possibility of throwing a perfect game. I can't think too much about it because that's the fastest way to jinx myself right out of the milestone.

"You fucking did it!" JJ yells as he jumps on me seconds after the umpire calls the batter out at home plate. I threw a perfect game. A feat only a handful of professional pitchers has ever done, and now my name will be added to that list. I hit the ground as the rest of my teammates pile onto the two of us.

"This calls for a celebration!" Matt O'Riley calls out as we head for the dugout.

I stop before walking down the stairs, and look up into the stands. Much like I do before the game starts, I seek out Jillian. She's standing, Penelope in her arms. I kiss my fingertips and hold them up in her direction. She wipes at her cheek before she repeats the motion. All I want to do in this moment is run up into the stands, pull her into my arms, and kiss the hell out of her. My teammate might have been on to something in his comment about celebrating, but the only person I want to celebrate tonight's victory with is the woman standing in the stands. The only one I care has my name and number on her back. She's the only one I'll be celebrating with tonight.

"Sorry, boys," I call out as I enter the locker room to cheers and congratulations. "I'll be celebrating at home tonight."

"Come on, man! Just one beer," JJ yells out from across the room.

"Maybe another night," I tell him as I strip off my jersey and toss it into the dirty hamper in the center of the room.

"Pussy whipped," he calls out. I can hear the humor filling his voice and know he's just giving me shit.

"Proud of it," I reply to the howls of our teammates.

It takes me over an hour to get through my shower and then the post-game interviews. All the media wanted to talk to me tonight after the performance I put on. By the time our PR people end the conference, I'm more than ready to get home to Jillian and the girls.

"Hi," Jillian greets me moments after I walk through the door. She's scrubbed her face of all makeup she had on today, changed into sweats and a faded Lightning t-shirt with my name on the back, and she couldn't look more beautiful.

"Hi, yourself." I pull her into my arms, nuzzling my nose into her neck. "Girls already in bed?" I ask, knowing they are for how quiet the house is and how late it is.

"Mhmmm." She hums as my lips coast along her jawline. "You were amazing out there tonight."

"I know," I murmur against her skin. "JJ was pissed I wouldn't go out with him, told him I had more important places to be."

"Is that so?" she asks, pulling back slightly so she can look up at me.

"Nowhere else I'd rather be, and no one I'd rather celebrate with tonight."

She nibbles on her bottom lip. "I've got a few ideas on how we can celebrate."

"Is that so?" I ask, hoisting her up onto the counter we've slowly walked to. I step between her legs as she wraps them around my torso, then bring my lips to meet hers, nipping at them. I could drink her in for hours if given the opportunity.

I sink my hands into her hair and angle her just so, then lower my lips back to hers as I take control of the kiss. I push my tongue past the seam of her lips and make love to her mouth, mimicking the way I'm going to make love to her once we finally get to our bed.

I pull away minutes—hell, it could be hours—later, as I've lost all semblance of time, and rest my forehead against hers. "Can you believe it, babe? A perfect fucking game!" I state, still in shock that it happened to me. That it's really my life.

"I can. It was amazing to watch. I'm so glad that everyone was there to see it happen in person."

"That was pretty special," I agree.

My cell starts buzzing in my pocket just then. I ignore it, but it starts buzzing again a few seconds later, as if whoever is calling me got my voicemail and called right back. I pull it from my pocket and see JJ calling. I decline his call, sending him to voicemail again, but he calls for a third time.

"Just answer it," Jillian says.

"This better be important," I bark into the phone.

"It's an emergency, dude. I don't know what the fuck to do," he rambles, so much I can hardly understand him.

"Slow down, what's going on?" All I can hear in the background is what sounds like a baby screaming. "Where are you?" I ask on second thought, putting the phone on speaker.

"Fuck, man. I'm freaking out. A chick I hooked up with last year just showed up on my doorstep with a baby in hand and said I was her dad. Said she couldn't raise the baby and left. What the hell am I going to do? I know jack shit about babies, and how do I even know if she's telling the truth?"

"Holy shit. JJ, calm down. I'm on my way," Jillian tells my best friend. She pushes me out of the way and hops off the counter.

"Dude, what the fuck," I say in shock. "Just hold tight, one of us will be over in a few." I hang up, then call after Jillian. "Babe, wait. Let me call Ry and see if she can come over here and stay with the girls, and we can go over together."

"Okay, but make it fast. God only knows what we're going to walk into over there."

I tap on my sister's contact and the phone starts ringing. "Hello?" she greets, a little groggy.

"Ry, sorry to call so late, but can you come over here? It's an emergency."

"What's wrong?" she yells into the phone.

"Well, JJ just called and said some chick dropped a baby off on his doorstep and left. Jillian was going to go over and help him, but I think it'd be best if both of us went. He's freaking the fuck out."

"Holy shit," she breathes. "Yeah, give me ten and I'll be over."

"Thanks." I hang up, and my head falls back as I look up at the ceiling. "I've warned him so many times that something like this was going to happen, but he never listens to me."

"I just can't believe someone would drop a baby off and walk away like that," Jill replies, sitting on the bar stool next to me.

"Are you sure you want to go? You can stay home, and I'll go, or I can take Ry with me," I offer. It's getting late and she needs her rest.

"That might not be a bad idea. We'll see what she says when she gets here. I don't want to volunteer her for that. She doesn't know JJ like I do."

"That's true."

A few seconds later, I see the flash of car headlights as Riley pulls into the driveway. I meet her at the door, and she walks in.

"I was thinking while waiting on you to get here. Would you actually be willing to just go with me? That way, Jillian can get off to bed?"

"I was actually thinking the same thing," she replies.

"Jillian, we're going to go. I'll text you with updates," I tell her as she joins Ry and me in the entryway.

"You sure you don't mind going?" Jillian asks Riley.

"Not at all. You go get some sleep. We'll go rescue the man child and the baby," she jokes.

"Good luck, and I want details," Jillian replies. I stop and take a moment to kiss her.

"I love you. And I promise we'll pick up where we were when we were interrupted later."

My sister slaps my arm. "Gross, I didn't need to hear that."

"Then don't listen to what I'm telling my wife," I snark at her.

"Then don't pull me out of bed to help with your idiot of a friend's emergency," she snaps back, a trace of humor in her voice.

"You've got me there." I kiss Jillian one last time before turning to head out the door.

We pull into JJ's driveway a few minutes later, since he lives in the same gated community we do.

"What took you so long to get here?" he asks as I open my truck door. I can hear a baby, a young one at that, crying from his open door.

"I called Riley to come stay with the girls, but then we decided she would come with me rather than Jillian."

He leads us into his house. "I have no idea what the fuck to do. Help!"

"First off, calm the fuck down, dude. Babies feed off of your stress," I tell him. We watch Riley hurry over to the car seat and pull the little baby from it. She looks to be about two, maybe three, months old, if my memory serves me correctly on what size my girls were at that age.

As soon as Riley cradles the baby in her arms, she immediately starts to calm down.

"What's her name?" Riley asks JJ.

"Um, Evelyn is what she said."

"Hi, Evie," my sister coos at the baby and she stops crying.

"Holy shit, you're the baby whisper," JJ says in astonishment.

"Not really," she says. "Did her mother leave you with anything? Bottles? Formula? Diapers? Clothes?"

"She left that bag." JJ points at a diaper bag sitting on his coffee table. "What the fuck am I supposed to do with a baby?"

We watch as Riley walks over to the bag and rummages through it. She pulls out a bottle and can of formula and walks to the kitchen, which is off the living room. She comes back a few minutes later with a bottle made and the baby sucking hungrily at it.

"Looks like she was hungry," she tells us as she takes a seat on the loveseat.

"So, do you have any information on the mother?" I ask a few moments later.

"Um, some," he says, running his hand through his hair. "Her name is Erica. We hooked up last year. She left me her cell number but said that she just couldn't do this on her own anymore and that it was my turn."

"That's pretty fucked up," I murmur. "I think, tomorrow, you need to call your attorney and get the ball rolling on a paternity test. Maybe try tracking down this Erica chick and finding out as much as you can about the baby."

"What am I going to do with her when I go to practice? Games? Road trips?" he asks, freaking out again.

"Well, if Erica is truly out of the picture, you're going to have to hire a nanny."

"I can help," Riley interjects. "I haven't found a job yet, so I'm available if you need the help."

"There you go. Problem solved for now," I tell JJ. "There isn't anyone we'd trust with our kids more than Riley. She's the perfect person to help you until you can figure shit out."

"Thanks," he says, blowing out a huge breath. "I still

can't believe that she just dumped the baby here and left. Who would do that kind of thing?"

"I don't know, but maybe it's for the best," I tell my best friend. Maybe this will make him change his ways.

"Do you have a guest bedroom?" Riley asks.

"Yeah, let me show you where it is." He stands and shows her down the hall, and I grab the diaper bag and follow. If she plans to stay here and help with the baby, at least for tonight, she's going to need whatever is in the bag. Jillian might need to run to the store first thing in the morning and stock him up on the essentials to get through the next few days with a baby in his care.

I feel like I'm more in the way than I am helpful, at this point. "Are you sure you're okay staying and helping out tonight?" I ask my sister when JJ leaves the room for a moment.

"Yeah, I'll be fine. He obviously knows shit about babies, so it isn't like we can leave him alone with her. I'll call you in the morning. I only saw the one can of formula and a few diapers, so we're going to need to run to the store in the morning," she tells me, confirming my earlier thought.

"I'll get Jillian on it in the morning. Text her a picture of the formula so that she can get the same kind, as well as the diapers."

She plops down on the bed. "Will do."

"Do you want this for her?" JJ asks, holding up the car seat.

"It's not recommended to let babies sleep in their seats but put it down over there, so I have it if I need it. I'll just be careful and have her sleep next to me. Tomorrow, we can get a pack and play or crib for her to sleep in."

"I'm so fucked," he says, pulling at his hair once again.

I've never seen him so stressed. "I don't know what I'd do if it wasn't for you guys."

"We'll get you through this," I tell him, slapping his back. "I'm going to get out of here. Call me if you need anything. I'll keep my phone on and next to me all night."

"Thanks," he says, the stress still rolling off of him.

"We'll be fine," Riley calls out, calm as can be.

TWENTY-EIGHT
DEREK

I MAKE IT HOME AND FIND JILLIAN FAST ASLEEP ON OUR bed. Her kindle rests on her chest, as if she fell asleep reading, which she probably did. Her cell is also next to her, like she was waiting on me to give her an update. I place both devices on her nightstand, making sure her phone is plugged in. I notice a text from Riley with pictures of the diapers and formula so we can get them for JJ in the morning.

I strip from my clothes, the exhaustion from the day and night finally catching up with me. It's after one in the morning, and my body is feeling it. I slide between the sheets, my hand finding Jillian's hip as I slip off to sleep.

"DEREK, WAKE UP," JILLIAN SAYS, SHAKING ME.

"What?" I ask groggily.

"What happened last night?" she asks, still in bed next to me.

I give her the quick rundown of last night's events and

she's shocked speechless. I tell her about the texts from Riley, and she hops out of bed so she can run to Target and load up on all things baby-related.

JJ: Dude, your wife and sister are lifesavers. I don't know how I'm going to ever repay them. Your wife showed up here about thirty minutes ago, with a SUV full of so much baby stuff it looks like a fucking Target exploded in my house.

Derek: Like I said last night, we're here for you, man. Let them help you. They know what they're doing. Just don't get any fucking ideas about my sister. I will kill you if you touch her.

JJ: I don't think I'll be touching another woman for a long fucking time at this point.

Derek: Don't say I didn't warn you; I know how you think when you let the head below your belt do the thinking.

JJ: Point taken. Now back to WTF am I going to do?! I'm not cut out to be someone's dad.

Derek: Take a deep breath and deal with it, man. Have you called your lawyer?

JJ: Yes, he's going to send over a lab company to swap for paternity. Said that the test takes a couple days to get the results. If they come back positive, he'll file the petition with the courts for temporary full custody. I gave him Erica's information that she left with me. Riley also found Evelyn's birth certificate and some other documents in the diaper bag, so we have that information as well.

Derek: Sounds like you've got things under control then.

JJ: If you say so.

Derek: Have you held her yet?"

JJ: They made me just a little bit ago. After Jillian got here, she changed her into a new outfit, and then handed her over to me for a little bit. I felt like I was going to break her.

Derek: I felt the same way when Addison was born. But you'll get used to it. Just take one day at a time.

JJ: I called Coach and told him what was going on. Told him I might need a couple personal days. He told me to keep him informed.

Derek: Are you going to go to practice this afternoon? I'm sure, between Riley and Jillian, they'll be more than happy to keep the baby.

JJ: I probably should. It would probably do me good to hit the gym and some balls today.

Derek: Then I'll see you there.

I toss my phone down and focus back on my own girls until Jillian returns home an hour or so later.

"How was it?" I ask her.

"He's so stressed out, but damn, is that baby cute. If I wasn't already pregnant, I'd totally have baby fever after seeing and holding her."

"How was Riley?"

"She was fine. She ran home to shower and change clothes. She packed a bag with some stuff so that if she ended up staying the night again, she'd have her things. I told her that we could get her her car later today."

"He's lucky she's able to just jump in and help him out like this. He'd be completely fucked if she wasn't here."

"I was thinking the same thing," Jillian muses. "Wouldn't it be super cute if they ended up together because of this?"

"Don't even joke about that. I already warned him not to get any ideas about touching my sister."

"Oh, come on now. She's a big girl."

"Not fucking happening," I grunt. "He's a manwhore."

"People can change."

"Still not fucking happening."

"We'll see," she singsongs, a smile on her face, like she knows something I don't.

The End!

Ready for Riley & JJ's story?
Read it now in The Curve Ball

COMING SOON

The Game Changer
Indianapolis Eagles Series Book 8
September 17, 2020
Add on Goodreads today!

Rumor Going 'Round
Lyrics & Love Series Book 3
Fall 2020
Add on Goodreads today!

ALSO BY SAMANTHA LIND

INDIANAPOLIS EAGLES SERIES

Just Say Yes

Scoring The Player

Playing For Keeps

Protecting Her Heart

Against The Boards

The First Intermission

The Hardest Shot

STANDALONE TITLES

Tempting Tessa

Until You ~ An Aurora Rose Reynolds Happily Ever Alpha
Crossover Novella

Until Her Smile ~ An Aurora Rose Reynolds Happily Ever
Alpha Crossover Novella

Cocky Doc ~ A Cocky Hero Club Novel

LYRICS & LOVE SERIES

Marry Me

Drunk Girl

INDIANAPOLIS LIGHTNING SERIES

The Perfect Pitch

The Curve Ball

ACKNOWLEDGMENTS

To everyone who has supported me, thank you! Thank You for the impact you have made on my life and my writing. Please know that I appreciate you all!

xoxo,
Samantha

ABOUT THE AUTHOR

Samantha Lind is a contemporary romance author. Having spent the first 27 years of her life in Alaska, she now calls Iowa home, where she lives with her husband and two sons. She enjoys spending time with her family, traveling, reading, watching hockey (Go Knights Go!), and listening to country music.

Connect with Samantha in the following places:
www.samanthalind.com
samanthalindauthor@outlook.com

Reader Group
Samantha Lind's Alpha Loving Ladies
Good Reads
https://goo.gl/t3R9Vm
Bookbub
https://goo.gl/4XyyLk
Newsletter
https://www.subscribepage.com/SLNL

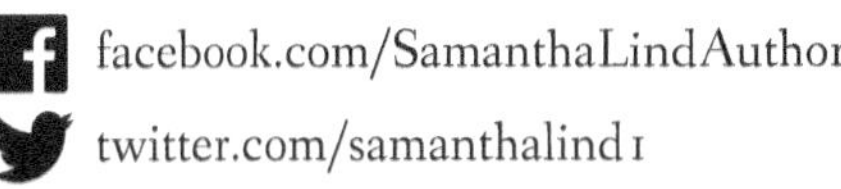

facebook.com/SamanthaLindAuthor

twitter.com/samanthalind1

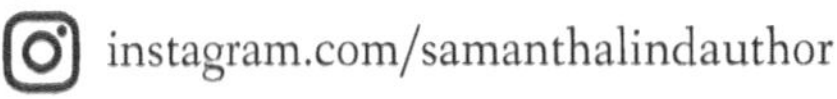

instagram.com/samanthalindauthor